ENJOY

PERISHABLES

PERISHABLES

The Withrow Chronicles
Book I

MICHAEL G. WILLIAMS

Falstaff Books

Cover Design by Natania Barron

Print Formatting by Susan H. Roddey, Clicking Keys
www.clickingkeys.com

ISBN: 978-1-946926-09-8

For more information on this or other Falstaff Books publications, visit www.FalstaffBooks.com.

Published by Falstaff Books
Charlotte, North Carolina
Printed in U.S.A

To Michael K., for bringing me back from the land of the dead.

The Vampire

W hen the zombies came, I was at a potluck for my neighborhood association.

Odd, isn't it? For all sorts of reasons, not just that I'm a vampire.

It's true, though, being there when the zombies showed up. I was ten minutes' walk from my place, down at the Reinholdts' five-bed, four-bath McMansion. Gods, but I hate that house. When they moved in we didn't have a neighborhood association to stop them from constructing that vinyl-sided monstrosity and no sooner had they dropped the last box in their front hall than they'd begun agitating to start one so they could make sure their place stayed the biggest house in the entire development.

Typical mortals.

Some of the more bothered types went and talked to lawyers or talked to the city or, in the case of Mr. Jones-Magnum - the only person who's been here so long even I have cause to fear his attentions - talked to the city in the presence of a lawyer and, eventually, everyone who cared shoved their hands in their pockets and slunk back up their drives in silent resignation. The Reinholdts knew how the game was played and immediately began campaigning for Best Neighbors Ever. With gift baskets and mown lawns and good candy on Halloween they whittled away just enough of the resentment against them that they got a neighborhood association started without being its first victims. By New Year 2002 it was a done deal: Franklin Not Frank Reinholdt was elected chair of the neighborhood association, with a three-member rotating board to keep the Reinholdts on a leash. Thus began their benevolent dictatorship of our neighborhood.

The neighborhood association's authority, I should note, does not extend to my yard. Oh, technically it does but Mary Lou Reinholdt always somehow seems to flinch when she tries to look me in the eye on my own turf. Every once in a while she'll come around and try to tell me one thing or another through the screen door but she always makes it fast and leaves faster. Franklin Not Frank won't even show up. He can't handle it. He's a wuss. The deal is, one of the rules imposed on the Reinholdts – really on Mary Lou, because we all know Franklin Not Frank is not the brains in that operation – is that whenever the neighborhood association considers a new restriction affecting a current homeowner's existing property then the homeowner has to be notified before the measure can be considered. The first time I actually met Mary Lou Reinholdt was for that very reason about four months after the association started.

Thirty minutes after sunset I'd heard a ring at my doorbell. I remember it took me a minute to figure out that it was, in fact, the doorbell. No one had rung my doorbell in years, not even on Halloween. I turn the lights on like anybody else but eventually my place acquired whatever psychic stain puts people of a mind to ignore it and move on. My guess is, I turn the porch lights on a little too late and I leave them on a *lot* too late and I'm never out mowing my lawn and people notice the little stuff like that. People don't notice the house that always stays the same so it fades into the background and they eventually learn to ignore the house where the dogs yap all day and the kids are always screaming but they notice the house that has a vibe of being just slightly off. A house that feels and looks too empty stands out like an open grave.

Anyway, the doorbell rang so I walked downstairs and peeked out the peephole and I could see Mary Lou standing there on the front porch with her lips pursed and her eyebrows knit together. She looked just as pissed as all get-out, *like how dare I not answer her*, and I figured she was a missionary or some other kind of low-life. I flung my door open so hard the hinges squealed and at the same time hit the whole bank of switches in the foyer so that the porch, front hall, front stairs and walkway were all suddenly flooded with the brightest, whitest light possible.

A vampire never gets tired of seeing surprise in a human's eyes.

"Mister..." She fumbled for a moment, and I made a show of studying her face while she did. I wanted to remember her but I also wanted her, whoever she was, to *know* that I remembered her.

"Surrett." I leaned my frame against the door and the floor creaked under me. I'll say it, I'm not afraid to: I'm a great big fat guy. I'm middling tall, about six feet if I remember correctly, but I weigh in somewhere around three fifty. I'd been out the night before, and just woke up, so I was in my black trench coat and wearing the boots that give me a little lift and my thick black hair was pointed eighteen directions at once because I hadn't hit the shower yet and she just stared and stammered.

"M... Mister..."

"Surrett," I said again. "Withrow Surrett. And I don't want no damn Bibles or newsletters or what-the-*hell*-ever, so get the *hell* off my land." I slammed the door shut and flipped all the lights back off with a smoothly reversed pinwheel sweep of the same arm. Mary Lou was left standing there just as blind as a bat. I could still see her out there as I stomped upstairs to get out of my club clothes and into something more reasonable, like the bath, and I smiled to myself because I could smell that she was a little bit afraid.

That's how I came to be a member of the neighborhood association's board. It was early. Some people were probably just getting home from work. Others were probably out on their porches enjoying the April evening. By whatever means, from whatever place, someone heard that exchange and the next month I got a note stuck in the screen door by an anonymous neighbor: a resolution to restrict the weight of dogs allowed as pets in the neighborhood had failed, and I had been elected to the association's board in absentia.

The dog thing was probably what Mary Lou came by to talk about. I've got a Doberman named Smiles. He weighs 150 pounds because I feed him some of my own blood once a week. When I have to go to town on my own, or when I leave him out front for the day to guard the place, I leave him on a chain that's too big for a large man to grasp in one hand because that's the only chain Smiles hasn't broken yet.

That got my attention, so I took the position on the board. What the hell, you know? Even we – *especially* we – can act on a whim and that was mine in that moment.

Being on the board turned out to be pretty low-impact. Once every six months I went to a potluck at the Reinholdts' damned house and we'd have a semblance of a meeting. I'd walk Smiles up there - no lead, I'd hate to see the leash that would work on him if he needed one - and drop him off in the Reinholdts' fenced back yard. He would spend the entire evening sitting on their back porch watching me through their series of French doors, ignoring their Jack Russell named "Killer". Killer usually just barked until he passed out.

The night the zombies showed up was the night of our spring meeting. It promised to be a pretty dull affair. The autumn meetings are always the ones where somebody gets pissed because their neighbor isn't raking enough for their liking or otherwise shit in the donuts and somebody needs to throw a hissy fit over it. Spring, on the other hand, is easy-going. Spring is when they're all dusting off that old landscaping software and talking about maybe *this* year they'll actually build those garden beds. It's a time when they imagine everything will be exactly the way each of them, individually, wants things to be all the time. As such, it usually involves nothing more fraught than a lot of sitting around munching on stale cheese balls and avoiding Franklin Not Frank's "world-famous" jellied beef loaf.

Don't ask. I don't even know what jellied beef loaf *is*. I asked one time and all I got in return was, "Oh, eh.... heh heh... think of it as a kind of *sausage*." Franklin has this weird vocal tic he only displays when I directly question something. It always starts with this half-hearted chuckle and then he avoids giving me a straight answer.

That particular spring it was remarkably warm - global warming has finally caught up with us, I guess - and we'd not had a single flake of snow the whole winter. Raleigh isn't exactly in the Alps but we're used to seeing a *little* winter weather. Not so that year, and we'd spent the first half of March with daytime highs in the 80's. As it was warm the night of the meeting I'd made do with some old jeans and a bright t-shirt with a picture of a cracked out kitten on the front. It was the sort of too-normal thing I liked to use to blend in but leave people a little wobbly at the same time.

Me and Smiles went up the street at an easy pace. I was bringing homemade biscuits and a batch of ambrosia salad. I love to cook, though I'm not particularly good at it. What tends to surprise most of my fellow kind is that I also love to eat. Most of us can't keep food down, our bodies reject it outright and it just comes back out, but my maker was a smarter one than most so she made me eat early and often to teach me how to keep it in long enough to fool folks. I was, as you might expect, not one to shy away from an ample meal in life and so I was glad to take up eating as a hobby in unlife. I might never lose another ounce of weight in all the time I spend on this earth but at least I can eat for hours and never *gain* an ounce, either. It's a small comfort, but with us every sensation counts.

When I got to the Reinholdts' place, I skipped ringing the doorbell and just walked Smiles right on around to the fenced back yard. The moment my hand touched the latch on their gate, Killer went ballistic.

Mary Lou knew by the sound that I must have arrived and came out on the back porch to greet us. She took one look at Killer and her shoulders sagged in a quiet sigh. For the first time in a long time I thought I detected something human in Mary Lou's body language but then the Stepford programming kicked back in and she smiled as best she could. "Withrow," she said, trying to purr and coming out sounding wrong. "So glad you could make it. I'm sure you're very busy."

"Oh yes," I responded, the ambrosia and the plate of biscuits cradled in my arms. Smiles sat by my feet and sniffed the air audibly in Mary Lou's direction. "Been working on a new manuscript."

"That's nice," she intoned, and then she turned and walked back inside, leaving the doors hanging open. She couldn't even handle that much small talk with me. It was nothing new.

A thought sometimes occurred to me in those moments when Mary Lou so visibly bristled at interaction with me: what if it wasn't just that I'd pissed her off that time on my porch? What if Mary Lou was one of those people who can just *tell* when something isn't right? What if every time I spoke she got those tingles up her spine that said, *That thing is not a human being?* There are vampires who believe that sort of sixth sense is out there, in folks whose great-great-great-grandfathers lived in one of our towns and somewhere along the line figured things out and now, generations later, they have scattered descendants who can simply *tell*, through some genetic memory or otherwise inherited gift, that something isn't right about us.

Me, I don't know what to think about that. I don't explicitly consider it impossible – I'm a *vampire*, I know a human being having something like a gut feeling about us is way down the list of crazy-ass things that can happen – but I've never known anyone for whom the possibility was a real concern. Mary Lou had made me start to give it more thought, though, and for all that my presence clearly made her a little unhappy I have to say the feeling was mutual.

About the manuscript thing - I'm a painter. Officially, my "grandfather" was the painter. *Officially*, I'm just an heir who releases the occasional found work and burns the proceeds to fund an utterly failed attempt at a career as a novelist. It's a shitty cover if you care what people think, but I don't care what people think. Mostly. Sometimes I care a lot. Pride is usually what gets us in the end, all of us, human or otherwise.

The rest of the board was there already and Franklin was busy talking sports with Kathy Sams and Herb Watanabe. Franklin isn't a sports buff, and neither is Herb beyond the usual water-cooler talk, but Kathy can't get her head out of it. Kathy played on the women's basketball team for one of the local colleges, back in the day, and she's a bigger sports nut than anyone you can think of. When I walked in she was busy haranguing Herb and Franklin over their picks for an office pool on the basketball tournament.

"Why the hell did you put Montana in as going to the Sweets? Have you ever watched Montana play? Every year they field the ten guys in the whole state who are over six feet and not busy throwing bales of hay across a field somewhere. This year they just got lucky!"

That's what I heard come from the living room. Herb Watanabe was trying to respond but Kathy was fed up with trying to explain it to him. Kathy officially considered the rest of us, who ranged from Herb, in the office pool because letting the boss take a few bucks from him was a way to fit in, to me, who couldn't care less without bursting a vessel from the effort, to be

8

lost causes. There was, she had said one time over dessert, something wrong with people who are so disconnected from their communities. Kathy's team in college had been good - very good - but this was before ESPN was giving a damn about women's sports. I don't have to be a sports fan to know that women get a lot more coverage these days, and that's a good thing, but Kathy was pretty bitter. She'd won a national championship but no one she met ever recognized her name

Kathy and Herb had become, over time, the only reasons I didn't walk from the board once the novelty of sticking it to the Reinholdts wore off. Well, OK, that's not true. The reason I didn't walk was because I still enjoyed sticking it to them even after it wasn't new anymore. Eventually I would've gotten tired of that, though. Probably. Kathy and Herb, on the other hand, they're good folks. They joined the board in part, I have come to realize, because they wanted to keep an eye on busybodies like the Reinholdts but in part because they also thought the HOA thing had potential. They were just people like anybody else, suspended in mid-air between a healthy dislike for pointless bureaucracy and sincere optimism about their efforts. I genuinely had no problem with them once I got to know them. I didn't exactly start sending them fruit baskets every Christmas but I had no reason to distrust them and couldn't manufacture a good reason to ignore them if I saw them out when I was walking Smiles, so I guess I have to say I liked them.

Dinner itself was the usual fare. We'd all brought a side dish and Mary Lou had done up a roast. Franklin had his jellied beef loaf out on the table and as usual everyone was kind of avoiding taking more than the amount exactly necessary for the sake of politeness. Conversation wound around the others' jobs - Herb is an architect, Kathy a programmer, Franklin does advertising jingles and Mary Lou is a property manager. Herb talked about how no one cares about good design, and the conversation briefly brushed up against how people these days just like to live in the biggest box they can squeeze onto a quarter-acre lot, but Kathy caught Mary Lou looking uncomfortable and so she steered us away into asking about Franklin's latest work. He'd supervised auditions for a campaign selling candy bars, and that was his big victory of the last six months: kids all over the country were humming a tune he'd picked for them whenever they stuck a dollar in a snack machine at school. Everyone stayed politely distant from probing me about my "professional" life, until Franklin said what he always says.

"Your grandfather was also an artist, wasn't he?"

I shrugged. "He certainly was."

"Quite a gifted landscape artist in his day," Franklin said to the others, as though he had to explain it to them every six months or they'd forget. I always hate this part of our conversations. Normally I sit there and let it happen around me but that night, for some reason, I spoke up.

"He worked in a lot of themes," I said without looking up from my plate. "Landscape was just to pay the rent."

"Oh," Franklin replied, trying to save face, "I didn't mean to imply that his art was limited, it's just that landscape is what he's known for."

"I didn't know anyone was known for landscape," Mary Lou said over her glass of blush. She smiled at me, and I looked up to meet her eyes. Mary Lou had a funny look on her face, and I thought again of that mythical sixth sense.

"John Turner," I said around a mouthful of broiled pork. "18th and 19th century. Hans Heysen, Monet, lots of well-known artists had or have landscapes as some of their best-known work. And it's still quite popular. There's Paul Sawyier, in Kentucky. Let's see, Kurt Jackson, he does mixed media sea-front stuff. Very impressive. Lots of stuff of Cornwall; he also does some photography." I shrugged and sat straighter in my chair, set my fork down on the plate, took a loud gulp of meat. "Landscape is a very respected theme, still, even if some people consider it 'fuddy-duddy.'" I stopped. I was starting to get pissed off, and my tone was showing it. I take a finished piece - one I've been careful to make using an aged canvas, a supply of paints it's hard to find anymore, timeline-appropriate brushes, all the things needed to produce a work that's effectively been counterfeited even though I really am Withrow Surrett and I really did paint it myself - and show it to a curator or a dealer and they check the signature and then they cluck their tongues and say something about how I was lucky to find it because surely there must not be many unknown works by my "grandfather" left and then they look at me like I'm the world's worst leech, like they can't believe I value my supposed ancestry so little as to place a high price on it.

Mary Lou arched her eyebrows and made an 'o' with her mouth. "I had no idea," she said. Everyone else chewed in silence. She made a little 'mm' noise to indicate she wasn't finished, like she'd just realized that perhaps she should clarify her statement. "I mean, I had no idea you were such an avid student of art, being a writer yourself."

"Well," I replied, "Fiction is an art."

"Yes," Mary Lou replied, so completely and blissfully tactful that no one could ever accuse her of trying to draw me out. "But there's a reason they call it 'arts *and letters*,' isn't there? I mean, there's an art to writing, yes, but they're not the same *thing*." She lifted an elbow to point it at her husband, gesturing casually with the same arm holding up her glass of wine. "It's not like writing *music*, or, say, painting."

I know what bait smells like, and I didn't bite even though I was definitely in the mood for it. Instead I just shrugged again. "Maybe so. I wouldn't know." Saying that was hard - the part of me that starved in a one-room apartment over an appliance store in Asheville for five years while I learned that landscapes are so important to the history of so many artists because landscapes will sit still long enough for you to practice your craft, to learn, to experiment, to compare the results of one technique with another, to learn the little inner cues that tell you when you're doing something right, when you should just keep working and not over-think it for a little bit because you've got that vibe; that part of me wanted to throw something. The part of me that has to maintain a public life just normal enough to go as unnoticed as possible, though, that part of me had to ride herd on everything else inside and it won.

Mary Lou was clearly trying to come up with something she could say in response to that non-reply, something that would cement her conversational victory, but I cut her off at the pass by jamming my fork into the sliver of jellied beef loaf I'd gotten and shoving the whole thing in my mouth.

No one had ever seen anyone else actually eat the jellied beef loaf before. Shocked silence descended on the table, and even Mary Lou's pupils dilated a hair's breadth when she saw me do it.

I chewed, and chewed, and chewed. Jellied beef loaf, it turns out, *is* a kind of sausage. Note the careful use of that phrase, though. Imagine taking deviled ham and stuffing it into a sausage skin, then baking it or frying it. It doesn't turn hard, but it's not complete mush. It tastes of salt and bland flesh, so there's nothing remarkable there. It's just meat-flavored stuff you put in your mouth and you chew. I was chewing a *lot* of it at once, and I chewed with merciless slowness. Chew. Chew.

Chew.

Franklin was watching to see what I thought, whereas Mary Lou and Kathy and Herb looked like they were waiting for me to topple over dead.

I swallowed the slice, raised both eyebrows slowly, and then lifted my hands over the table. I was very careful to give the impression that I was either going to reach for other food or I was going to try to cover my mouth before projectile vomiting. I let that second or three stretch out, and then I reached for the plate with the rest of the jellied beef loaf on it, carved a generous length of it and lifted it onto my plate.

"Delicious, Franklin." I nodded at him, and then smiled. "I had no idea."

I picked up the entire severed portion, one long and greasy tube of dull beige-pink, and bit it off like a candy bar. "Mmmmm," I said, tonelessly, still smiling. I took another elaborately slow bite. "Yes," I went on, rolling it around my palate, pausing to let the bouquet express itself, then jawing it again. "Delicious."

After that, Kathy eventually picked back up the mantle of conversation and wore that yoke through the rest of dinner. She tried to talk about the artistic side of programming - elegant designs, smooth operations, helpful commenting - and tried to use that to tie into writing in an attempt to build a bridge between me and Mary Lou. Herb helped her out as best he could, and over time it turned into Franklin and Herb and Kathy talking about how corporate structures obscure the creative efforts of the individuals in their employ, no matter how creative any one of them is, even if every individual in the organization is trying to be creative. As they turned into the Bad Luck Club, grousing convivially about the hardships of cubicle farms, Mary Lou kept watching me eat as I finished off the rest of the plate of jellied beef loaf. If Mary Lou was onto me, if she wanted to watch me for whatever it was that raised the hair on the back of her neck, I was happy to give her something innocuously bizarre: a taste for jellied beef loaf. I even smeared some on a biscuit and ate it like *pâté* to keep her on her toes. I smiled the entire time.

Franklin had just asked Herb and Kathy if they were ready for him to bring out dessert and they had made the appropriate noises about how it was too much but they'd love to try a little when I realized two things: Herb and Kathy were lovers and that I'd just heard a car accident in the distance.

I doubt it will surprise you to learn that vampires have remarkably keen senses. I heard screeching tires and a car horn and then the distinctive tin can crunch of metal against an obstacle and I could tell from the sound that it was probably three blocks away.

No one else had heard it at first, so when I looked up and around towards the windows at the front of the house and the street beyond the others all started in surprise.

"Hear something?" Kathy asked. The slight tremor in her voice told me she and Herb and Franklin had grown weary spending the last fifteen minutes walking on eggs. She was jumpy.

I looked at her for a moment and nodded towards the window. "Thought I heard something, but it could just be my imagination." The others looked towards the windows, too, even Mary Lou, and then I heard the horn again.

"Was that a car?" Franklin looked out in that general direction.

"I..." I paused, considered, went on. "I'd swear I heard a car accident just a second ago." I set down the last of the current biscuit. "But, you know, it could be anything." I looked the other direction at the French doors off the dining room and Smiles was still sitting there watching me. He's a pretty good gauge of when weird stuff's going down, but he can also be misleading. His only job is to protect me. If people are dead in the street he doesn't really give a damn unless I'm one of them. Killer, on the other hand, forgot Smiles just long enough to run to the fence and start yapping his head off.

The car horn sounded again, closer this time, and then headlights splayed against the front of the house. The horn was more insistent than before, and

Franklin walked to the front windows to survey what he could see beyond the shrubs they'd placed there for privacy. "Someone's just pulled up in the drive," he announced.

I knew that something very bad was about to happen because from outside I could hear Smiles start to growl.

I wasn't going to start crazy paranoia talk out of the blue so I sat at the table and watched the living room and foyer. Franklin stood in the bay windows, watching the car in the driveway, and narrated for us as the guy got out of his car and ran up the front walk to the door.

"What's he look like," Mary Lou asked, and Franklin shrugged at her in the dramatic, both hands out to the side, both shoulders pumping up and down way of an actor on stage.

"He's just some guy," Franklin said, but it was cut off by the doorbell ringing frantically: RING-A-RING RING-A-RING RING-A-RING, and then the guy started beating on the front door and shouting something we couldn't make out.

"Aren't you going to answer it?" Mary Lou had stood from the table and was trying to shout over the noise, Franklin looking back at her uncertainly. His hand hadn't moved from the blinds; he hadn't moved from the window. "*Answer it*," Mary Lou shouted, and Franklin took two hesitating steps to the door. In those few seconds, the guy's shouts had become less complicated and more coherent. Whatever he was yelling before was just a muffled jumble of syllables, but now it was easy to make out: *Help me, there's been an accident*, he was saying. *Help me, please; I need to call the police.*

Kathy and Herb were still sitting at the table with me, and I noticed that they had briefly touched hands under the table, both looking to the other for reassurance. Definitely lovers. They weren't going to do anything, and it didn't look like Franklin would either. I started to stand up, my napkin falling out of my lap and into the middle of my plate, but Mary Lou had already made for the door. The guy was still tap-dancing on the doorbell so I couldn't make out what Mary Lou said to her husband as she went by him but it was ugly and her face was set as hard as an anvil. With one twist of the knob and a practiced sweep of her other hand she'd undone the dead bolt and yanked the front door open. The stylized, decorative ukulele on the back of it - tiny, with three strings instead of four, little wooden spheres suspended on twine such that they would bang against the strings when the door opened - twanged a wild chord and the others all jumped a little in anticipation of what they might see.

The stranger on their doorstep was, in fact, just some guy. He was in his late 20's or early 30's, dressed in khaki slacks and a solid-color oxford button-up. His close-cropped black hair and his coffee-colored skin cooperated to make him look a little younger than he might actually be, and his wide, red eyes and choked speech indicated that whatever had happened out there, he had just now started sobbing over it. His head was turned away from the house, in the direction he'd come, but when the door opened he whipped back around and stared at Mary Lou, lips quivering, for a long moment before he said anything.

"Holy fuck," he mumbled, his voice strangled and high-pitched. "Oh, god, we have to call an ambulance, I just ran some guy over in the street." Other than his voice reaching for the top end of the scale and shaking wildly, he sounded pretty together. Shock, I figured. Turned out I was right, because he interrupted Mary Lou when she started to say something in response: "But..." He shook his head at her and she was quiet. "But then it happened *again*," he said.

We all blinked at once.

"Franklin." Mary Lou was very calm. "Go and get the telephone and call 911." Franklin was quick to obey, and disappeared into the kitchen immediately. Mary Lou had never taken her eyes off the kid at the door, and this time he let her talk. "Now," she said, voice even, "Tell me exactly what happened so that we can help you." She reached out and took the kid's elbow and led him out of the doorway, into the foyer, and closed and locked the door behind him. He sank into an armless chair between two large, fake plants - a chair I'm pretty sure Mary Lou would only let someone use in the event of an emergency, so the kid at least had that going for him - and took two deep, ragged breaths. "Actually, first," Mary Lou added, "Have you checked on either of them? Do they need first aid?"

The kid shook his head and his eyes went wild all of a sudden, his pupils wide like saucers and the whites bulging out at me. Trust me when I say that I know the look of mortal terror on a human being. This was *that*, and everyone in the room recognized it from firsthand experience or from ancestral memory.

It's interesting, actually, there's been research done on this. There is an evolutionary advantage in people looking all crazy when they're real scared. One article about it said, basically, that it's how cavemen knew when someone was coming up behind them. Bottom line, when one person sees another person do that - eyes wide, pupils dilated, whites of their eyes just all over the place - it produces fear in the observer as well as the observed. It triggers the fight-or-flight mechanism.

It does not trigger that in vampires because a lot of the basic human instincts simply shut down after the Big Bite. That doesn't mean it gives us a warm fuzzy, though. In the movies, it's always Dracula running around with that stupid grin, his fangs hanging out like a TV antenna got stuck in his windpipe, people screaming up and down the countryside. It isn't like that for us, not really. We - well, the smart ones, anyway - try to avoid creating fear as much as possible. Fear gets people talking. Fear makes it hard to keep something secret and it makes people overreact. When humans start shuffling around and looking to each other for guidance we start hoping they've got their torches and pitchforks well out of reach. Fear makes people do *crazy* things.

"No, they don't need first aid," the kid said, shaking his head. I wondered what the hell was taking Franklin so long with 911. "No, they..." The kid threw his hands up to his face and pushed back the skin around his eyes. "They're dead," he mumbled. "And... they look dead. They look... *really* dead." We were sitting in silence, and then the kid went on after a second or two. "They look like they've been dead a *long, long time.*"

Kathy and Herb both held their breath, and Mary Lou wrinkled up her forehead. "What do you mean?"

"I mean they were corpses," he said after a second. "I mean there were corpses in the street."

"Dead bodies in the *street?*" The Mary Lou Reinholdt that asked this question was not one human being concerned for another; she was the wife of the president of the London Towne neighborhood association.

"Dead bodies... walking around," the kid said, and then he turned to one side and puked his guts out all over one of Mary Lou's plastic plants.

Franklin chose that moment to emerge from the kitchen. "I called 911; they said the police would be here soon." He looked at all of us, looked at the kid trying to wipe his mouth on his sleeve, looked back at Mary Lou. "They said they were already close by, so it would be quick?" Franklin's expression was one of confusion and bewilderment. Mary Lou looked down at the stranger, then up at Franklin and made a motion with one hand, against her other arm. I realized she was trying to mime injecting something. She thought the kid was drug-addled.

"OK," she said to him, taking a step back, and Franklin doing the same, very casually. "So what's your name?"

"Jeremy," he coughed.

"Jeremy," Mary Lou said very gently, "We've called the police, and they're on their way to help. In the meantime, I think if we go outside and look again you're going to find that you've imagined something very terrible and it's shaken you up very badly." Mary folded her hands together in front of her. "Do you want to go outside and check?"

Jeremy looked at her with his red-rimmed eyes and then looked over to the door and shook his head violently. "No way, lady, no way," he panted. "No way am I going back out there."

"Well, Jeremy, that's up to you." Mary Lou was 110% condescension. "I'm going to go see, and I'll be right back." Before anyone could say anything - though Franklin did at least open his mouth for just a moment - she'd whipped the front door back open and gone out, pulling it shut behind her.

Kathy and Herb were looking intently at one another, both hands still clasped under the corner of the dining room table, and I could hear Smiles growling again outside. Killer was barking his stupid little walnut of a brain out. No one noticed as I slipped in perfect silence out the French doors onto the back porch. I may be a lumbering fat-ass but any vampire worth his salt at least knows his way around some gauzy curtains and a simple door latch.

The back yard was silent for a moment when I stepped outside – Killer ceased his yapping just long enough to look at me, and Smiles' growl stopped as soon as I was in his presence again. For those few seconds I closed my eyes and opened my ears and let my senses roll out across the yard, then over the fence and into the adjacent lots, on out across the neighborhood. I could hear televisions in several houses, a cough that sounded like it wouldn't get better anytime soon – had to be Old Lady Jenkins, the one with all the in-home care – a couple of radios tuned to a local call-in request show.

I could hear soft footsteps on grass, someone shifting their feet back and forth.

I could hear shuffling, shoes scuffing against asphalt as though a drunken man were staggering down the street.

And another.

And another.

Very softly, I could hear Mary Lou praying under her breath.

I opened my eyes, and the night was gone. Darkness is no enemy of mine, and these old eyes can slice right through it. Smiles was watching me, waiting patiently for a command. I signaled him to stay and went out the gate to the front yard.

Mary Lou was standing at the curb, on the grass, looking one way and then another and shifting her weight between her feet. Her lips were moving but I don't think she was exactly in charge of what was coming out. Fight or flight is not an instinct many people are really at home with anymore in their insulated little lives.

I strode up and cleared my throat from about six feet back. Mary Lou whipped around with wide eyes, took a moment to recognize me, then turned back and looked mutely up the street. I took two more steps to stand beside her, and followed her gaze.

Three corpses in their one-time Sunday best were staggering mindlessly in small circles in the middle of the street. They were probably thirty, maybe forty feet away. If they had noticed us yet they didn't have much in the way of showing it. They just turned and turned and turned again, arms stiff by their sides, hands clenching and unclenching reflexively.

You'll not mind I don't describe their faces.

"Whu..." Mary Lou was outside the mind of someone who could form words for the moment.

It is said that there are stranger things in heaven and earth, et cetera, and they ain't kidding. I know the world holds some esoteric and arcane shit because I'm one of those things myself but I had never seen the dead literally walk. I mean, we've all seen the movies, right? I have, anyway. Shit, for a solid three decades all I had to watch at night were old movies on UHF channels. These fellows weren't exactly *Night of the Living Dead* and weren't exactly *Frankenstein*. No one could confuse them for a mutant or a junkie on a bad batch. They were dead things, plain and simple, walking around. They did not moan, they did not hiss or howl, they just turned in slow circles, around and around, their eyes locked in front of them.

"Go inside," I said to Mary, very softly. "Just go inside. Lock the door behind you."

She still wasn't very capable of listening and just stood there. I started to get antsy – surely they would notice us eventually, right? Surely they would sense we were here: smell us or hear us or see us or something. They were dead, yeah, but in the movies that's always how it happens, right? Someone screams and then the zombies all stop what they're doing, turn slowly and charge. I really didn't want to be in that scene of the movie. I always hated those parts the worst, when some idiot loses their shit and gets everyone else killed.

I put my hand around Mary Lou's chin and turned her head so that she looked me in the eye. With all the force of personality I could muster, I bored my mind into hers and said, very distinctly, "Go inside and lock the door and let no one inside." There's a reason why the Count always gets what he wants when he's alone with somebody in the vampire flicks. Mary foggily turned around and started stumbling back towards her front door.

I watched her go, checking over my shoulder to see if the three walkers up the road had heard us or anything, and as she neared the front door she reached for the knob. The door opened before she got there, though, and Franklin Not Frank poked his head out.

"EVERYTHING OKAY OUT HERE?" he called to me, unnecessarily loudly. He was scared and wanted to demonstrate to everyone that everything was precisely OK out here.

I heard the scuffling in the street stop, and turned around to look. None of the walkers were looking at me, but they had turned towards the house, and the front door, and the source of the shout. They started shuffling towards the house and their stiff arms started to twitch.

I will kill that man before they do, I swear to God, I thought. What I said, however, was yelled over my shoulder. "Get her in there and shut that fucking door!"

"Well, there's no need for," Franklin started to say, but Mary was still under my orders and she shoved him back inside, followed after him, shut the door calmly – absently – behind herself, and I heard the deadbolt slam home. That was something, at least.

The walkers were making achingly slow progress – in five seconds they got about as many feet – and so I clicked my cheeks twice. Smiles jumped the Reinholdts' fence from a sitting start and bounded up to my side. "Guard," I said, and Smiles braced himself on all fours, eyes on the lead walker, a growl starting to climb the stairs way down in the bottom of his chest.

Picture the scene for a moment, if you will: a suburban McMansion squats on an otherwise '60s-ish street. The house itself is mammoth and beige and appears to have been dispensed from a machine designed to manufacture the word "dull" made manifest. A morbidly obese guy in blue jeans and a kitten t-shirt is standing there with his arms crossed over his chest. A Rottweiler two sizes too big is standing next to him, ready for a fight. A droplet of pink foam is at one corner of the dog's mouth. It growls deeply, like a bone saw dropped three octaves. There are three obviously dead people in black suits walking towards them. Their arms twitch. Their hands clutch at the air. Their faces are expressionless because their faces aren't really there anymore. In the distance, a small dog is working its heart out to sustain a crescendo of barking. A man is shouting questions inside the house behind them. The walkers come painfully slowly down the street, shoes dragging, one of them barely able to walk for what appears to be a crushed hip – he's injured in a way that for a living thing might spell death but he's still moving under his own power.

They approach to twenty feet.

They approach to fifteen.

The fat man draws a breath.

I was, I want to note, ready to fight. I would have killed all three of them – again, I guess – right out in the street in front of God and the neighborhood association's executive board and everybody. I could answer their questions later. I could come up with a story about a martial arts class I'd signed up for, a home gym I'd bought, some semi-plausible reason why a guy who looks like me would know that much about hand-to-hand combat. I drew one great breath and flexed every muscle in my body and heard my heart jerk in my chest so that it said THA-DUP, very loudly, and old blood started to push through my veins. Blood does many things for my kind. Hearing a heartbeat, even our own fake one, can do wonders for morale.

The lead walker got within ten feet of me and I kicked out one leg so that I was standing with my feet spread, one forward of the other, hands open, arms bent at the elbow. I was ready to pounce, and Smiles had shifted his weight so that his front was crouching and his ass was in the air, ready to do the same. His growl was a powerful and steady grating, and I started to growl, myself, the two of us ready to kill.

The lead walker got within five feet of me and stopped suddenly, then wheeled and started shuffling more quickly in the other direction.

I blinked, and Smiles' growl ceased for a moment.

The leader stumbled right past the other two, got about ten feet, and then started doing circles again.

The other two likewise got within five feet of us, spun around and headed in other directions.

I relaxed for a moment, and watched them. Smiles wasn't going to move until I gave him another command, so I stepped gingerly around to my right and forward in a great arc, keeping about ten feet between me and the lead walker.

Then I stepped within five feet of him, and he tore off – as best he could – in the opposite direction.

I tried it again with one of the other two and got the same results.

The walking dead, I realized, were afraid of me.

One of the ones I'd spooked made the mistake of staggering within a couple of feet of Smiles and my old dog was quick to react: he had the guy's throat in his teeth before I could make a sound and two seconds later Smiles was standing on its chest. I heard bones snap and the walker's head popped clean off, rolling a few feet before bumping against the curb.

The body was limp under Smiles, and he stood there growling at the corpse's head where it came to rest.

So they feared me, but not my dog.

I thought about this just long enough to realize it before a phrase I hate to think on over-much came to mind, unbidden: "food chain."

I gave Smiles the command to heel, as anxious as he was to go after the other two walkers, and I gave the fear and revulsion I felt for these things a few seconds to subside. Deep breaths are calming even when your lungs are just for show. I let their aimless, stumbling presence in the street settle into my view. I did my best to calm myself and then I opened up my senses again and let them wash out over the neighborhood.

Televisions and radios were still playing in other houses. Either the neighborhood didn't know about these things yet or it was too late for those folks. They weren't my primary concern, anyway; I wanted to know if there were more of them. I could hear the two nearby, of course, and I could hear Smiles' accelerated breath, and I could hear voices inside Franklin and Mary Lou's house – sounded like they were still doing some arguing in there.

Underneath it all, I could still hear scuffling feet, farther away, old dress shoes dragged across asphalt in all directions. The neighborhood was full of these things, I'd have guessed a dozen or more, and I needed to decide now whether to deal with them myself or wait for help to arrive.

My reverie was broken when I heard glass shatter around the back of the house, and the two walkers in the street stopped and turned in that direction. Two seconds later, screams erupted from inside, and I sicced Smiles on one of the walkers while I ran down another. With a single punch I popped the head and neck off of mine and Smiles had taken the other one out at the knees.

"Here," I commanded, and Smiles let go of it to come bounding after me. All three and a half bucks of me were moving as fast as I could make them go, and in a flash I had kicked the front door in with one foot and was stepping inside with the other. Smiles shot past and dug his claws into the hardwoods to stop a few feet in front of me, eyes forward. I glanced around to see what the hell was happening. Kathy and Herb were in each other's arms in the middle of the living room and Mary Lou and Franklin and the new kid, Jeremy, were pressed against the stairs, cowering.

A walker was standing in the dining room, its feet hung in those gauzy drapes on the French doors. What was left of Killer, I am not terribly sad to say, was clutched in one hand and the walker was reaching forward with the other, fingers twitching, clawing at the air to try to pull free of those drapes. Everyone was screaming all at once. I grimaced and slammed the door shut behind me.

"STAY," I bellowed, as Smiles shook his flanks, about to lunge. I strode forward, shoved Kathy and Herb down behind the coffee table, walked around the couch into the dining room and stopped at the other end of the table from the walker.

Its eyes fell on me and it snarled.

You ever watched two dogs that were playing all of a sudden get into a real fight? They're just having a normal time and then one growls the wrong way and the other answers, instinctively?

I bent a little at the knees, clenched my fists and did something I should never have done in front of another living being: my lips curled out of the way so that my fangs could drop down and I growled, long and low, and every light flickered for a moment and every shadow got just a little darker.

All the screaming stopped, like a switch, and Smiles started barking as I leapt, knowing the walker would just try to run if I got closer, knocking the table to one side and going straight for that one outstretched arm. I grabbed it near the elbow in both hands, the walker emitting something like a strangled scream. With one long, arced motion I had wrenched it free of the drapes, gotten it airborne and brought its back down over one knee with an unmistakable splintering sound. On the rebound I caught its neck in my hands, planted my shoe against its spine and tugged hard until I heard that pop I'd heard outside. I hefted the head back through the broken glass of the door and threw the body after it.

I turned back around and everyone was staring at me.

"You're gonna want to theal thethe windowth," I said.

Everyone was silent and pale – even Jeremy, whose skin had gone from creamed coffee to a sick beige – and I checked myself.

I was lisping.

My fangs were still out.

The next twenty minutes were filled with busy silence, except for my voice. I'd withdrawn my fangs the moment I'd realized I was still showing them, and then started barking orders. People who are in the early stages of shock just want to be told what to do, and I took full advantage of that. Kathy and Herb got the food off the table and then lifted it up into place in front of the broken back door. Franklin and Mary Lou told me their kids were out of town for a school trip and wouldn't be back for two more days. I then put them on door-fixing duty. When I kicked it open I'd blown the deadbolt out and across the room, so I had them digging a little bathroom throw-bolt out of a cabinet and affixing it to the front door for all the good it would do.

Jeremy, the new kid, was useless. He'd seen too much in too short a time. Between hitting a couple of them with his car and all this jazz in the house he'd gone catatonic. I didn't hassle him, didn't even try to give him a job to keep him occupied. Instead I stood in the middle of the living room, where I could keep an eye on my newest soldiers, and flipped my cell phone open.

Vampires are, as a rule, fairly solitary creatures. Still, like in any subgroup, there is a culture of sorts. We don't totally get in each other's business, we don't do a lot of socializing, but a hierarchy always asserts itself in any given place where there's more than one of us. Here, I'm at the top of that hierarchy. I make the rules and I enforce the rules.

As the local boss I have to have a couple of lieutenants, biters who can help me keep a sense of what's going on around town. Seth is the best of these: a taciturn punk who's never shown much interest in discussing his life story. He keeps his nose clean and tells me when there's trouble, like if someone's come around from other parts and doesn't keep their business tidy, that sort of thing, and that's really the best I can hope for from any of us. The most valuable thing one vampire can offer another is to leave them the hell alone and not make any trouble.

Seth's the bartender at a club downtown. The owner's a lush, too drunk to notice that Seth's looked twenty-five for the last fifteen years. They have a deal worked out about Seth sending a friend – some kid he pays on the side – to take care of receiving deliveries during the day. The lush doesn't care who signs for the packages, and Seth makes sure the place's inventory doesn't go missing, and everybody's nice and happy.

I dialed Seth, knowing he'd be serving the tail end of the office drunks and getting ready for the start of the college-kid rush. His phone rang twice, and then he snapped it open:

"I could use a hand if you're bored," he said, voice low.

"You at work?"

"Along with a few customers, yeah."

"I take it you're boxed in?"

"Don't tell me this shit's happening all the way up in the suburbs," Seth said. We were both silent for a few seconds. If it was happening here, and it was happening downtown, it was everywhere.

"I've got my hands full, too," I whispered into the phone. "I can't come lend a hand. I was hoping you would do that for me, actually."

"Are you safe?"

I paused. What answer did the 2nd in command want to hear?

"Eh," I replied. "How are the cops?"

"We saw a bunch, lots of sirens and speeding earlier. Haven't seen anything in a while. The scanner's pretty quiet."

"It'll take them a while to get here, I take it."

"Probably."

I sighed, and then said, "Keep safe."

"Yeah."

We hung up at the same time.

I watched over the others as they worked. It took them a while to dig up that lock and manage to get it on the door. They fumbled with it, swore at it, wiped rivulets of sweat from their brow as they did so. Kathy and Herb, meanwhile, were moving more furniture into place to barricade the French doors in the dining room. It wasn't perfect, but nothing ever is. This was the best we could do.

After that, I gave a few quiet but equally stern orders for them to get the food up, check what was still edible, then put it away in the fridge and the freezer. The power was on and we didn't have any idea how long they would be trapped here so I wanted them maximizing the use of what resources they had. I went through the pantry and did a quick inventory check - typical suburbanite fair, lots of prepared foods and almost nothing raw or that really required heat to be eaten. If they had a can-opener, and they did, they could live for weeks on the stores of their massive walk-in. I was a little jealous and a little disgusted all at the same time. My ultra-frugal mother would have died if she'd lived to see it.

And finally, after forty five minutes or maybe an hour, when it was getting on towards eleven and there wasn't a whole lot I could think of to make them do, they sat down wearily in the living room and broke into obvious couples and just held each other in silence.

"I'm gonna step out front for a smoke," I said, my voice quiet. "You slide this new lock behind me and only let me and Smiles back in, alright?" Franklin nodded absently, so I walked out with Smiles at my side and dug a bent cigarette out of my pocket and lit it. The little bolt lock clacked behind me and I let out the first drag in a long, slow stream through my nose. So far so good, but I knew as sure as anything that sooner or later, and probably sooner, one of them was going to ask the obvious question: what the fuck am I?

Of course, the sooner the cops got here, the better. Then I could just leave and blame any questions on the obvious craziness of the whole night. "You must've been seeing things," is something I have said on more than one occasion and it's worked. Sometimes I've had to put a little oomph behind it, a little hoodoo, but it doesn't exactly work like that on crowds. I'd never been in a situation like this before: up close and personal, with a bunch of my neighbors, in a stressful situation in which I am the only one capable of really defending myself?

They are fucked, I thought.

I got through one smoke and then lit another. What? It's not like I'm going to die of cancer, is it? As I worked on the second, Smiles was sitting alert by my side, sniffing the air, and I closed my eyes to let my ears go walking. I could hear more walkers, in the distance - more than I'd heard before. I wondered where they were coming from, what had made them? This is the South and we have graveyards *everywhere*. There were probably thousands - hundreds of thousands, maybe millions - of potential walkers within a hundred miles of Raleigh. How long would this last? What was tomorrow night going to be like? These are the sorts of things I was thinking to myself, and finally I finished my second butt and let my mind come back to the here and now.

Well, I thought, *No time like the present to make a better world.* With that, I set off up the front path. "I'll be back in a few," I called over my shoulder, loud, so they'd hear me inside. No point being subtle given what I was going to do.

I was going to clean up the neighborhood.

The first walkers I ran into were standing in the front yard of the house next door. It took me and Smiles all of ten seconds to dispatch them. I then strode up to the front door and rang the bell, hammering on the door with my other hand, calling out. No answer. The lights were on, and I peeked through the blinds in the front to see the sliding glass door at the back of the house, shattered, a drape torn down from in front of it. There were corpses inside, but fresh ones, not moving. OK, so there was already a body count. I beat on the door again, got nothing, then kicked it in so hard the hinges snapped and it flew across the entryway. That got something's attention, but it was a walker. I took him out fast, annoyed that I was having to do a little crab-walk to cut them off as soon as I got close enough to make them run the other direction.

I moved across the street, checked that house and started working my way out across the neighborhood in a spiral.

By midnight I'd gone a two-house-wide circle around the Reinholdts, and swung back by. They didn't answer when I called to them from the door but I caught the whole crew - Kathy, Herb, Mary Lou and Franklin but not Jeremy - watching me from the living room window as I left again to continue my patrol.

Our neighborhood was built a few decades ago, but it's grown again here and there over the years. The way I figured, I had a couple hundred houses to check, the pool and clubhouse, the playground and a small city park that backed up against the back of our development. It would keep me busy at least and it would keep me from being around the Reinholdts' place to answer any questions.

I figured they were probably suspicious of me by now - scared, shocked, the usual. They were probably debating what to do about me. I didn't mind giving them some time to work that out in my absence.

While I was out working my way through the neighborhood I called 911 a few more times. I never got an answer, just a 'please wait and your call will be answered' message. I didn't even know 911 could *do* that. I checked in with Seth and he was getting the same, though he'd seen more cops out since we'd spoken the first time. It sounded to him like they were doing the same thing I was doing - just trying to make a sweep and kill as many as they could find, then turn around and do it again. Every time he saw a siren, he heard gunfire. He and his clientele were holed up at the bar, biding their time. They didn't have much in the way of food but they had a whole bar's worth of liquor and that was all the drunks really cared about.

By the time I'd gone door-to-door through the whole neighborhood it was three in the morning. I hoped the crew back at the Reinholdts' place was asleep by now. On the other hand, how could they sleep? I hoped most of all that none of them had decided to try to run for it. Any one of them on his or her own would be dead meat in front of a walker.

As for the neighborhood, it wasn't pretty. Most people were either not answering or their house had obviously been intruded upon. A few people were willing to call out to me from upstairs windows, but only a very few. Most of those were willing enough to exchange a few quiet words, ask if I'd seen the cops, all the predictable stuff, but some of them just shouted at me to get away, stay away, leave them alone. They were scared shitless and I was a stranger to most of them. I'm sure they'd all seen the name on my mailbox but very, very few of these people had ever seen *me* despite my having lived here since the '60s and most of these people not even having been born then.

At the last house, which was another collection of victims, I tore open their garage door and dug a can of yellow paint and a brush out of a cabinet.

28

Wielding that, I started to work backwards through the neighborhood, marking houses as I went. The city park and the clubhouse and the pool could take care of themselves. For now, I had houses to mark. If the occupants had been unresponsive and I'd confirmed a corpse inside, I painted a big X on the front door. If there were living people inside, I painted "OK" in big letters. On most houses I painted a question mark.

It took me three more hours to work my way back to the Reinholdts. Surely by now they'd have settled on how to handle me or they'd all be asleep. Either way, I figured I'd at least gotten to skip the melodrama. I found a few new walkers on the way back, and that told me that wherever they were coming from, there were still more coming.

It was just before 6:00 AM when Smiles and I walked back up the front walk of the Reinholdts' house. The sky was just starting to turn blue instead of black on the eastern edge, and I knew it wasn't going to be long before I had to get inside. My house was just a few minutes' walk and these walkers were nothing to me. I could have gotten to my house on time if I'd had to wade knee-deep through them the whole way there.

To tell the truth, a part of me wanted to do just that. The same part of me that pulled at its chain when the walker in their dining room groaned at me, the part that made me just sweep the table aside and pull its head off with my bare hands, that part of me wanted to turn around and go home and say fuck it, they can all die. On the other hand, a part of me felt a tiny little twinge of guilt for having left them here rather than take them with me - though of course that would have been a terrible mistake. Guilt rarely listens to reason, though, so I set down the can of paint, raised my right hand and knocked hard on the front door.

"It's Withrow. I'm back."

It was quiet inside, and I started to worry, so I knocked again. I called out louder. "I've been around the neighborhood. I've cleaned up the ones I could find out in the open. I've checked in with everybody who'd answer the door. C'mon, I just want to make sure you're OK and then I'm going home."

Still silent.

I looked down at Smiles and he was busy watching behind us, sniffing the air again. I took that as a good sign, but still, I had to know for sure. I clicked my cheeks at him and the two of us went around back to the barricaded French doors. I clambered over them and into the dining room.

Mary Lou was sitting on the couch, an enormous handgun across her lap. The others were sound asleep, snoring to beat the band, huddled in the middle of the floor. I was kind of surprised that I hadn't woken them but I also noticed a prescription bottle on the coffee table: sleeping pills, a brand I've seen advertised on TV. Vampires are real good at knowing when someone's alive and someone isn't, and when they're in a bad way, and I could also tell that none of them were breathing heavily or laboriously. They hadn't tried to do anything stupid, they'd just made sure they could sleep, except for Mary Lou: awake, exhausted but alert, standing guard over them. I'd bet in an instant that she was the one who'd organized them and made them get some rest.

"What are you?" she said, very quietly. For a second I was afraid the gun was meant for me, but she didn't put a hand on it. She just had it sitting nearby, her hands together in her lap, fingers intertwined to keep from fidgeting. She didn't even look at me.

"You know what I am," I sighed and eased into a recliner. Smiles padded around the sleepers in the floor, climbed into my lap and put his head down on my arm. "The real question, of course, is whether you're going to do anything about it."

"When you left," Mary Lou said, "We were terrified. We sat up talking about it for a long time."

"I figured as much."

"You went off and gave us time to talk about you?"

I shrugged. "Yeah. What'd you decide?"

"They…" She nodded at the sleepers, stifled a yawn, gulped out of a big mug of coffee. "Didn't decide anything. They're useless." She sighed quietly. I arched my eyebrows. She still wasn't looking at me, and there were tears in her eyes, but there was a hardness there that hadn't been present when she knocked at my door all those months ago. "No, they talked and talked and talked. No one would *say* it, of course, so they just talked around it."

"The 'v' word," I murmured.

She nodded, still staring out the window.

"Lots of 'is it safe to have someone like him in the neighborhood,' lots of starting to ask the obvious questions and then stopping because no one wanted to be the one to say it."

I drew a breath and said, "What are the obvious questions? Pretend I don't know."

"Oh," She rubbed her eyes. "You know, what does he eat? Does he turn other people into... what *he* is when he does it. What's he going to do to us now that we know? All that stuff."

I nodded, and stroked the fur behind Smiles ears. He made a little brrowr of pleasure and snuggled in.

"Oh, and of course they think your dog is Satanic."

I smiled a little, but I meant what I said. "I don't advise anyone try to mess with my dog."

"Typical," she sighed. "Where did you grow up? It had to be in the country, with an accent and an attitude like that."

"I don't generally like to discuss my life," I replied. Also, the small talk was a way to avoid something, and I couldn't tell what it was.

"OK," she said, and she lifted one shoulder in an exhausted shrug. "We sat in silence for a few moments, and then I patted Smiles to get him to stand up and climb down off my lap. "Looks like you've got things under control," I said. "I'm gonna go home." Mary Lou didn't seem interested in responding at first.

"You didn't ask what *I* had decided to do about you," she said as I stood.

I sat back down. "That's true."

"You don't care what I think?"

I opened my mouth to reply with: *It doesn't matter what you think,* but I stopped. Now probably wasn't the time. Instead I remained neutral. "What did you decide?" I asked.

"At first I wanted you gone. I wanted you out of our neighborhood. I wanted to call the cops and tell them... I don't know. Yesterday if I'd called them and told them a vampire lives in my neighborhood, you wouldn't be the one they took away. Now? Everything is different now, isn't it? Assuming there are even cops to call." She rubbed her eyes again. "Then I realized that I was terrified - not terrified *of* you, though that was true at first. No, what scared me was something altogether different. I was scared that you wouldn't come back, that we would be on our own. I could herd them into submission on the easy stuff - convince them to make themselves sleep rather than have to sit up all night listening to them go over and over and over what to do with you. But I'm not sure I can pick up this gun and shoot one of those... things. You know, if it tried to come in the back door or something? Franklin is here, and I suppose if it threatened him then I'd have to but I don't *know*. All I know is that they run from you. I watched the one in the dining room try to do it. I watched the ones in the neighbor's yard do it. You went out for hours, on foot, unarmed, and you came back without a scratch. You've knocked on every door in the neighborhood. You've killed how many of those things? Don't actually answer that. You did it without a thought. I'm sure I could tuck you away in a midnight movie definition if I needed to, just like I can with the things outside, but that's not the point. The point is that I was scared you wouldn't come back."

"I appreciate your concern," I said quietly. "But you don't need to worry about me."

"Oh, I wasn't thinking about you," she sighed.

The silence in the house, other than the snoring, was heavy. The silence out in the street was heavy. Usually, when I'd be bedding down right about now, I'd already be hearing a few cars: the paper delivery, the first early-risers headed out to beat the morning traffic. All of that was absent. All I could hear outside, now, were birds. It occurred to me none of us had tried to turn on the news, see what the hell was happening. It was like the second we saw *them* everything went out the window: all normalcy, all reason. Now Mary Lou wanted me to stick around and protect them when she was the one who'd managed to put them together, get them talking, get them to *sleep*, loaded a gun and sat up all night watching over them. She didn't need me. She just needed to keep doing what she was doing.

"I've got my own house to worry about," I finally said. "And others to think about."

She swung her eyes around at me at last. "Others like you?"

"I..." I rubbed my eyes. The clock said 6:07. I had fifteen minutes to get back home. "No. But people, all the same."

"You're lying," she said quietly. "There have to be others like you. I imagine you all know each other. I bet you all know all about each other, keep an eye on each other. You'd want to know if each other were in trouble. You took a call earlier. I bet that was one of them. Are they here? Do they know whether this is everywhere? I imagine it is. It must be, or the police would have come by now."

I chewed my thumbnail for a moment. "It's here and it's downtown and that's all I know. I need to get home. Turn on CNN and see for yourself."

Mary Lou blinked at that suggestion, then reached over and picked up the remote. A click, and the TV came on; another, and she had muted it, turned on the closed captioning. She turned to a local station - now would be the early newscast - and a disheveled redhead woman who wasn't the usual anchor was talking into the camera. Behind her right shoulder there were scenes of fires, of emergency crews, of a National Guard truck rolling down Capitol Boulevard. The shot cut to some police officers gunning down an advancing wave of walkers but the station had, in its eternal propriety, blurred them so we wouldn't have to look at those not-faces. The captioning read:

I REPEAT, POLICE ARE WORKING THEIR WAY THROUGH THE CITY AND EXPECT TODAY TO REACH THE NORTHERN AND SOUTHERN EXTREMITIES OF CITY LIMITS. IF THEY KNOCK AT YOUR DOOR, PLEASE CALL OUT CLEARLY TO ANSWER THEM. THEY WILL HAVE SOME EMERGENCY SUPPLIES ON HAND, INCLUDING FIRST AID MATERIALS. IF YOU DO NOT ANSWER, THEY MAY ENTER TO SEARCH FOR HOSTILE AGENTS.

"House to house?" I said, surprised. "Goddamn, that can't be legal."
"You just did it."
I glared at Mary Lou for a second. "I ain't the police."
She looked back at me, and raised both eyebrows in disbelief. "That makes it better?"

"I did it because I care," I said.

"You care so much you'll leave me here by myself?"

"Oh, Mary Lou," I said, because I had finally had it with just that tiny bit, "Get over it. You've got a gun the size of a Howitzer and four grown people to help. The five of you might shit your pants when you do it but you could take one of those things in two seconds if you worked together. I may be strong and fast and tough but I'm no five adults who are high on adrenaline. You are going to be fine. Just..." I spread my hands in frustration. Had people really gotten that weak? Were they that timid? Was I like this, sixty years ago? "Just get the fuck over it, already."

"Easy for you to say," she snapped, her eyes hard, her lips thin and tight. "They *run* from you. They didn't eat your *dog*. They didn't walk out in front of your *car*. They didn't break down your back *door*. Oh, yes," and now she was practically hissing, "It's very easy indeed for you to say. What's a few more monsters when you're one yourself?"

My eyes widened, just a little. I realized Smiles had awakened, and was watching her in silence. She looked at me, then at him, then threw her hands up and let them flop down on the couch beside her. "Oh, yes, very easy; very easy, indeed. Maybe they were right. Maybe your dog *is* Satanic. Maybe *you're* a demon. Fuck if I know. All I know is what I see on *Buffy*. Maybe you're just cowards. Maybe you're all just terrible cowards, slinking through the shadows and *feeding* off what you can, scurrying off the second the light gets shined on what you are, like cockroaches with thumbs." She turned back to the TV, where the warning about the house-to-house searches was being repeated. "Well go, then. Go and have a lot of fun when the cops show up at your house today and they call out and you're... I don't know, in your coffin? Buried in the earth? Who knows? Go right ahead and let them knock your goddamn door in when you don't answer and let them shoot your dog and tag you as just another corpse because if you can just walk away from five people who want your help - who need your help and *want* your help and how often does someone like *you* hear that *anyway* - then I don't know what you are and I don't *want* to know." She reached up and brushed a tear aside, and then punched the pillow beside her on the couch.

None of what she said was what kept me from stomping out in a blind rage

34

and taking a door with me so they'd all learn what happened when they pissed me off. It was that TV news broadcast, and those words being repeated every thirty seconds or so in big, block letters in the closed captioning: IF YOU DO NOT ANSWER, THEY MAY ENTER.

If the cops came in and found me during the day, either I'd never wake up and they'd think I was a body and when I came to I'd have a whole mess of questions to answer; or Smiles would kill them; or I'd wake up and likely kill them in confusion. Day sleep is not like normal people sleep. It's like hitting a brick wall. You close your eyes and you're just *out*.

Mary Lou, for all her self-righteousness, was right. I'd never make it if the cops came into my house and I knew myself that when they knocked I'd never answer.

"I'll stay," I said heavily. "But I have to have a dark room. Really dark. I don't mean dim, I mean pitch black, preferably a closet or an interior bathroom where I can stuff a bunch of shit under the door. It has to happen in the next ten minutes or I'll set this whole house on fire when the sun catches me." It was the most direct discussion of the nature of my biological state that I'd had with anyone since the night my maker turned me free.

Mary Lou was staring at me, kind of stunned I'd actually agreed or said all that or anything. I realized instantly that she hadn't really blamed me and she didn't really want a vampire as her benevolent protector. She was just angry, and sick of it, and scared, and I was there to be yelled at. But after a few seconds she set the gun on the coffee table and nodded. "OK. Let's get you in the guest bath. It's going to be cramped."

"Any port in a storm," I sighed. "But do not, no matter what, open the door during the day. Trust me."

"Alright," she said. "I can make sure that doesn't happen."

"Smiles is going to keep watch outside the door." We were walking up the steps and she grabbed some towels out of a linen closet, handing them to me. "It's what he does. Nothing in the world will change it. I'm not even sure *I* could get him not to. So, nobody comes near the bathroom. He'll go for anybody he perceives as a threat to me and he knows during the day that I'm vulnerable."

Mary Lou nodded, opened the door of the guest bath and gestured for me to enter. I started towards the door but she looked puzzled and said, "So why didn't he go for me when I was yelling at you?"

"We're... bonded." I said. "It's complicated. Bottom line, he didn't do anything because I didn't feel threatened."

She looked blank for a moment, so I said it: "I could take you, gun and all, if I had to. OK? Your curiosity satisfied now?" Then I signaled Smiles to sit in the hallway, eased into the bathroom, closed the door, stuffed two towels under it and settled into the tub. Before I'd even rested my head against the tile the day sleep had me and I was gone.

My eyes snapped open the moment the sun dipped behind the horizon and the last of its light left the world.

My sleep was uneasy. When I'm at home, I can sleep well past sunset if I let myself. I was always a deep sleeper, and some of that quality remained after the big flush. These were unusual surroundings, though, uncomfortable and cold and quiet in a way other than the usual quiet of my own home. The hum of the central air was different, the white noise of electronics. As soon as my eyes opened and I remembered why I was in someone else's bathroom I rose and rubbed my eyes and clicked my cheeks. Smiles barked once in response from the other side of the door.

So far so good.

I smoothed my hair down as best I could, poked around in the drawers and cabinets and found a little bottle of mouthwash. I swigged it, spat it in the sink and splashed some water on my face. Then I yanked the towels out from under the door and opened it. Smiles licked my fingers and panted happily, and I listened down the hall, down the stairs, to check for indicators of how the day had gone.

Nothing.

I walked out into the hall, to the top of the stairs, put my hand on the railing and started to descend. There was a quiet gasp from the living room. I guessed at least one of them had managed to survive the day.

When I got to the bottom they were all awake and alert; they were even eating leftovers from the night before. Mary Lou looked at me for a long second, then at the others, and I followed her gaze. They were all staring at me like they'd seen a ghost.

"I told them what you did on your patrol," Mary Lou said. "The cops figured out your code pretty quickly. They said..." She paused, and cleared her throat. "We're the best-organized neighborhood they've seen so far. They were very grateful."

There was something in the tone of her voice when she said 'grateful,' and after a second I got it: the cops were grateful, Mary Lou was grateful, but someone wasn't and she was trying to rebuke them like a mother in front of company.

"The rest of you want me out." I stated it as an epilogue to her update. Kathy and Herb wouldn't look at me. Franklin looked to Mary Lou then back. I met his gaze. "*You*, specifically, want me out. Fair enough. It's your house."

"Well, uh... heh heh..." Franklin did that same little verbal tic again. "It's not that we aren't gra--"

I didn't let him finish. "You're glad to be alive but scared that I'm more dangerous than anything I might have saved you from. You don't know what I am and that terrifies you. Well, welcome to the human fucking race," I said. "Ain't nothing new that hasn't scared us shitless. Trust me. I remember a lot more of this world than you do."

"I can't believe you'd say 'us,'" Kathy murmured.

I glanced at her then looked back at Mary Lou. "Fuck this," I said. "I appreciate the use of your bathroom. I appreciate you doing like I asked and not messing with me during the day. I appreciate the food from last night, and now I'm going the fuck home because I don't appreciate being talked to like that."

"I'll see you out," Mary Lou said. She stood up and walked to the front door, threw back the makeshift bolt I'd had them put on, turned the knob and walked out ahead of me. I pulled the door shut behind me.

"Give me a cigarette," she said.

I raised one eyebrow, then nodded at her. She'd changed clothes, taken a shower, done her hair, put on makeup. Mary Lou was getting back to normal real fucking fast compared to the rest of the sad sacks in there. Jeremy was still catatonic and the rest were barely moving. I held out my pack, open, and then lit her cig and followed it with one of my own.

"They gonna do me any harm?" I asked.

Mary Lou laughed quietly, under her breath. "I thought you could take them," she said.

"That I can," I replied, "does not in fact mean that I *want* to."

"OK. That's something." She wouldn't look me in the eye but that had made her think.

We smoked in silence for a minute, then I said, "So what's the state of things?"

"The news has no idea what these things are. I mean, everybody knows, but no one's going to come out and say *zombies*. I watched a little Fox for a laugh. They think it's an elaborate terrorist attack. It was contained to just a few places as far as they can tell. The city's mostly been swept clean. They said on the six o'clock news that most of them were found in graveyards, obviously, but that they hadn't gone anywhere. They were hostile but not... purposeful. The estimated toll is pretty high, but it's not like half the city is gone." Mary Lou nodded her head towards the back of the neighborhood. "It turns out the park back there used to be a graveyard."

"And the contractors didn't move the bodies they got paid to move," I finished for her. "Happens all the time."

Mary Lou nodded, shrugged. "Nothing's open, the governor and president declared states of emergency, no one is going to work, no one should go anywhere except for emergency supplies, that kind of thing." She shrugged half-heartedly. "It's starting to sound less like an attack by the walking dead and more like a really bad hurricane." She laughed suddenly and shook her head. "It's fucked up. Can you believe they handled zombies better than they handled Katrina?"

"Hell yes I can," I said. "A bunch of white folks in suburbia? The government's quick to help us, I'm sure." I sighed, and stubbed out my cigarette on her front step, then lit another. "That's good, though, that people are thinking of it that way. The sooner people just file this away in their brains as something bizarre but temporary, the sooner we can get back to normal."

Mary Lou finished her own cigarette in silence then put it out very delicately and, while she was doing so, picked up the butt of mine and stuck them in her pocket. "I'll take them in," she said. So here she was, even making sure I didn't litter in her yard. I guessed she'd be okay after all. "But," she went on, "About going back to normal..."

I nodded and stuck my thumb towards the inside of her house. "They're all still wigged out."

"Yeah."

"About me."

She nodded.

"I can fix it, you know." I sighed and rubbed my free hand through my hair.

"That would be a good thing," Mary Lou said.

"Alright. I'll need to see each of them one by one, and they'll need to go straight home when I'm done with them."

"Including Franklin," she said. At first I thought she was asking me not to put her husband in a more agreeable frame of mind, but she wasn't. She was requesting that I be sure to include him.

I nodded. "And you?"

"No," she said. "That's the other condition. I'll put them out here on the stoop with you, one at a time, and I'll keep them busy so the rest don't notice, and in return you let me remember."

I chewed my thumbnail, blew smoke through my nose, and then nodded. "OK."

She went back inside and sent Ken out first. He walked out carrying a broom. I had no idea how she'd convinced him to go sweep her front step, but I had folded myself into the corner behind the front door, the porch lights off, and when he stepped out I reached around, gripped his shoulders, spun him, looked him deep in his terrified eyes and made it all better again. A minute later he was walking down the street, entirely certain that we had all spent the night and the day hiding and protecting one another, that I had gone out and checked on a few houses, yes, and that I had slept all day because I'd been up all night on guard duty but that there was nothing remarkable about me at all.

Then Kathy.

Then Franklin, whom I ordered to go upstairs and go to sleep.

Then the new kid, Jeremy, who was starting to come out of the catatonic state and looked terrified of all of us. I sent him back inside to go to sleep, too.

And then I walked back in the front door. Mary Lou was standing there with the gun and she shook her head when I started to reach for her shoulder. "This wasn't the deal," she said. "You said you wouldn't mess with my head."

"I lied."

"I'll shoot you."

"Won't matter, except it'll be a shame to lose this t-shirt after all these years."

"I'll shoot the dog."

I cocked my head at her and made a pffffft noise. "Won't matter except it'll piss him off real bad."

I pushed some blood around so that the world slowed down, reached out in a blur too fast for her to see and took the gun from Mary Lou's hands, shoving it between the cushions of the couch. From her perspective, I knew, the gun would simply have disappeared in a flash of movement of my left arm.

She gasped, and her eyes started to water up, and she shook her head. "Please," she said. "Don't mess with me. Not my mind. Not that."

I spread my hands out to either side. "The way of the world, Mary Lou. It's got to be done."

"Will I forget you?"

"No, just certain information."

"Will I think of you differently? Will I wake up tomorrow thinking you're a swell guy or will I still be allowed to think you're a deadbeat snob and a bully?"

I blinked. "That's what you think?"

Mary Lou cleared her throat.

I sighed and crossed my arms. "Ask me a question," I said.

She blinked and sniffled and looked confused. "What?"

"Ask me anything you want to know. You knew I was an odd duck before any of this happened. You had a sense that something wasn't right over dinner. You felt it for the first time when you knocked at my door that time, years ago. You've been thinking about this, and you've probably got questions. So ask one."

Mary Lou blinked again and drew a couple of short breaths. It was just me and her again, everyone else gone about the business I had assigned them after rearranging their minds to my advantage.

"Are you your grandfather? Are you the painter?"

I rolled my eyes. "Yes, obviously, and that's so obvious it doesn't fucking count. Ask me a real question."

She laughed all of a sudden and rubbed her hand across her face, looking around. "Uh..." She paused, and said, "Will you paint a portrait of our family?"

"No," I said. "Too easy to fingerprint as mine. It would be a chronological idiosyncrasy. We don't allow those. Again, too obvious." I leaned my fat ass against the back of her couch. Smiles was snuffling happily around the parquet floor in the entryway.

Mary Lou thought for a few seconds, then drew herself up and looked me in the eye. "When you drove away the one in the dining room, and when you made me come back inside, and when you went out around the neighborhood and checked every house; did you do that for our good, for theirs? Or did you do that to protect your... turf?"

"Yes," I said. "Yes I did."

I reached out to take her jaw in my left hand and force her eyes to mine but she stepped back. "One more question." I paused. "Don't you want a friend?"

I blinked at her and smiled just a tad - the corners of my mouth twisted up, ever so slightly, my eyes half-lidded. "Come on," I replied. "Let's take a walk."

It took us ten minutes to walk to my house, neither of us speaking the entire way. Smiles trotted along next to us, sniffing the curb and growling at the tracks of a downed walker here or there. Mary Lou was calm but clearly wary of being out and about. There weren't any problems, though, and in the distance we could see the occasional blue and red flash of a patrol car's lights.

We went up the front steps and onto my porch in the dark, her hand on my arm so she wouldn't stumble, and I unlocked the front door, had her wait while I disarmed the security system, and then I hit that bank of light switches with that same sweeping motion so that the yard and the house were lit up like the 4th of July.

"Come in," I said over my shoulder. Smiles was home again, and glad of it, and he bounded into the kitchen and practically dove into his bowl and started crunching happily.

Me, I went on my usual circuit of the downstairs - left into the dining room, on into the kitchen, a glance out the sliding glass door, then to the right, crossing the end of the front hall, into the den, then right again into the sitting room. Everything was exactly as I'd left it. There were, I noted, a couple of bloody handprints on the sliding glass door. I pay good money for bulletproof glass, though, and no walker was going to get through there with a couple of slaps and what gumption it could muster. It had moved on, I imagined, to some easier target.

I had very consciously left Mary Lou behind to absorb things at her own pace. My place is nothing particularly special - I tend to keep myself in comfort, but I'm not extravagant and my house is one of the oldest in the neighborhood. She peeked into the dining room, starting off at first just following me, but in the kitchen she stopped and watched Smiles eat his chow for a few moments, then looked out onto the back deck. I watched her note the handprints also. Then she glanced into the sitting room and walked into the den. Her eyes were not on my furniture, or the carpet, or the general decor - the furniture and carpet were new ten years ago and decor is Standard American Suburban, neutral walls, neutral carpet, earth-toned couch and matching chair and a sturdy wooden coffee table. The TV is big, but not fancy. It, too, was new ten years ago.

The thing she was looking at, or at least I thought so at first, was that everywhere on the walls I'd put up my own art: landscapes and portraiture and a few impressionistic pieces I'd done over the years, a few examples of cubist knock-off, that kind of thing. As far as I was concerned, this art was all the equivalent of the everyday china - not special, not the kind you mention in the will, but nice enough to look at. I wondered if she were impressed, or horrified, or annoyed, or what? I stood in the doorway, having returned from my cursory downstairs sweep, and watched her as she stood in the center of the den and turned in a circle and looked it all up and down, every wall.

"Where are the pictures?" she asked.

"Pictures?"

"Photos. You know. Friends... family?" Mary Lou cleared her throat. "It seems lonely." She paused again. "Generic."

"This from a woman with a modern marvel squatting on top of a quarter-acre lot."

"What do you mean by that?" Her voice was immediately defensive, and I sighed in reply.

"I don't keep photos around."

"So that part's true?"

"I don't follow you."

Mary Lou had the decency to blush a little. "That part of the movies? You can't have your picture taken?"

I frowned. My patience was wearing thin. Mary Lou had not gotten the point. I decided to deliver it myself, and in a motion had crossed the eight feet between us and wrapped one fat hand around her throat, leaning in close. "I do not keep photos because that sort of life is over for me," I whispered. "Get this, Mary Lou Reinholdt. You wanted to know if I wanted a friend? You thought I would bring you here and we'd have tea and cookies and play patty-cake and then you'd leave and I'd let you remember everything and you'd get to pretend you'd done me a favor?"

Mary made a squeaking noise and I relaxed my grip very slightly so she could breathe. Then I pulled her a centimeter closer.

"Mary Lou," I whispered, "Let me be clear: I don't *want* a friend. Friendship does not mean the same thing to me as it does to you. Kindness has a different definition for me than it does for you. You want to come here and make nice and try to integrate *me* into *your* view of how your safe little world works. You don't like that you relied on me for your safety earlier, that for a moment you people weren't in control, that you were *weak*, and so you want to be able to just file me away as a friendly weirdo." I turned my head and spat blood-foam against the window that overlooked the fenced back yard. "It isn't like that, Mary Lou. I am *different*. I am *me*. I wanted you to come here to see that. Yes, I have a couch and cable TV and a dog but my dog is part devil and my couch is only ever going to have one worn spot on it and I don't keep photos of my friends around because we don't exactly take beach trips together. My life is not *like* yours." I started walking towards the kitchen, dragging her with me, and turned her so she could see the refrigerator. I hooked the door handle with one thumb and tugged it open.

"You see that?" I asked. "Top shelf: food and drink. The three shelves under that?" I paused. "Those are blood bags, Mary Lou. I am a different kind of creature. I *will not* be domesticated. I *cannot* be domesticated." Her eyes were wide and she was producing little gasping noises again, so I let go altogether save for one turn of her shoulder to point her at the sliding glass door. I pointed one finger at the bloody handprints. "Those were made by an animal, and you don't *like* animals. You don't like Smiles because somewhere deep in your lizard brain you have a fear reaction to him. You don't like me because you get the same case of the willies when I'm around. When you saw those first couple of walkers out in the street, you froze because they were outwardly Other. But me?" I met her eyes with mine as she turned to look at me in abject terror. "I have a *face*, and I have *eyes*, and I can join you for dinner and make nice conversation if I need to, and that's *worse* for you, somehow. But rather than just accept that, rather than accept that I've lived in this neighborhood for fifty years without bothering anybody in it, rather than just let me be me and you be you and go our separate ways, you have to *try* to be *friends*. Well, save it for the status-conscious gay Republican who moves in down the street one day, or the black couple that feel uncomfortable around a bunch of crackers like us. Save it for whatever inescapably different people - emphasis on *people*, Mary Lou - move in here one day. Don't waste it on me. Don't try to put me on a leash or box me up the way you did with Smiles." Again, I leaned in close, and whispered into her ear: "And don't think you can sit there in your living room with your big-ass gun and some *moxie* and best me like some mindless *thing*. We are different animals altogether - them and me, and me and you. We're as far apart as you are from them, Mary Lou, and I want you to know that, to remember that deep down somewhere, maybe in a recurring nightmare, maybe in a chill that runs up your spine the next time we have a neighborhood association meeting and I walk in the room, however your subconscious chooses to tuck it away, just remember that."

I paused to draw one more long breath.

"You were impressed that I went out among them and fought back last night because you have never been invaded. I moved out here fifty years ago, way outside of town, to get away from you animals only to have a bunch of other hermits show up out of nowhere. Then the developers invaded and built houses all around us and paved the streets and put in streetlights. Then you showed up and invaded the invaders. Now the city is trying to move in on you by running sewer lines and annexing us. Last night was just one more wave in a series for me, Mary Lou. It simply happened to be a lot more honest than the previous ones."

She was digging her fingers into the edge of the counter on the island in the middle of my kitchen, behind her back, trying to fight the urge to cower against it. I stood back and looked her in the eye. "You arrogant piece of shit," she said, and I confess I respected her for it.

Then I reached into her mind and made her forget.

Fifteen minutes later she was asleep in her bed, next to her husband. I'd walked her back - she would later remember this as an adventurous and slightly terrifying jaunt we'd taken together to see whether my house was safe - and made sure she was inside. Their kids would be home the next day, assuming the cops and the Guard lifted the travel restrictions in and out of the city. I let myself out the front door, locking the knob and pulling it shut behind me. Smiles and I had a spring in our step as we went up the street.

I could see the flicker of TVs in some of the houses, including some with my big, yellow X's on the doors; TVs were still on where their owners had died. Life goes on, even with a corpse on the couch. There were lights in some of the ones without the X's, too, and from those I could hear quiet voices, the sounds of normalcy struggling for a foothold in the face of something bizarre and inexplicable and inescapable.

I rounded the curve where West End met Buckingham and turned right up the sidewalk towards my own house. A cop standing next to a police cruiser swung around at the sound of my footsteps and shined his flashlight in my face, bright. I tossed a hand up to block my eyes and said, "Goddamn!" He took the light out of my face and shined it at Smiles, then dropped the beam to the ground and leaned into the radio on his shoulder.

"S4 to S3, encounter, investigating."

A squawk answered, and the cop stepped forward. "Can I help you, sir?"

"Just headed to my house," I said. "I live up this street. Spent last night and today with some folks from the neighborhood."

The cop eyed us both, then nodded, gesturing with the flashlight. "I'll radio you ahead. Please go directly home. If you need emergency supplies, a Red Cross van will be through this development at noon tomorrow."

"Thanks, but I'm all stocked up," I replied, and I turned to go back the way I had been headed.

"S4 to S3," the cop said into his radio, "Had a live one, provided direction, over." An affirmative crackle put the cop back in his normal, watchful pose.

A live one, I thought. I heard that cop's voice over and over again in my head as I walked the rest of the way home: A live one, he'd said.

A live one.

EDIBLE INTERLUDE

Powdered Ambrosia

Ambrosia Salad has been around since the late 19th century and is a Southern staple on the church social and family reunion circuits. Withrow has eaten mountains of the stuff over the decades and one can find a million recipes online. Its component parts might be hard to find in the event of societal collapse but with a little creativity one can produce a passable variant. Better living through science!

- 1 package spray-dried full-fat powdered heavy cream
- 1 package spray-dried full-fat coconut milk
- 1 can shaved coconut (optional)
- 1 can (8oz) fruit cocktail, drained of water/syrup
- 1 can (8oz) pineapple chunks, drained
- 1 can (11oz) mandarin oranges, drained
- 1 jar or tin of ground nutmeg
- 1 jar or tin of ground cinnamon

All of these ingredients have one major advantage: they can be found in the warehouse of any restaurant supplier, a business to which most people won't think to turn in desperation. The powdered heavy cream and coconut milk in particular will almost always *only* be findable on the shelves of a commercial wholesaler.

Prepare a significant quantity of heavy cream using the liquid from the canned fruit instead of water but otherwise as per package directions. If you have the coconut milk powder you can mix the powder directly into the resulting cream; it will sweeten the cream and give it body without needing to find sugar. Whisk the cream (or mixture) vigorously for several minutes until it becomes frothy and starts to stiffen. If you have powered tools available, use a hand mixer or stand mixer.

Mix in the drained, canned fruit and stir to distribute evenly. Sprinkle a couple of tablespoons of nutmeg and cinnamon on top and stir again to incorporate it. Top with shaved coconut and consume immediately. Due to the fat content of the powdered cream this could go rancid in a few hours if left unrefrigerated.

THE COLLEGE TOWN

My boyfriend told me that moving to Mt. Ares was going to be a mistake I would "rue." Can you believe that? Nobody says "rue," nobody but characters played by Jeremy Irons. That's what I told him, too, when he said that. I threw back my head and laughed at him and told him he was being stupid. I knew he was right, though. I knew I would hate living full time in a do-nothing little town like that so… I didn't.

Instead, I kept my rattrap in Asheville and did a lot of commuting to Mt. Ares, 45 minutes straight up the side of a mountain. It made for some wonky hours, some really early mornings I didn't enjoy, but it meant I got to have a life. If I'd actually gone and lived up there I'd have been schlepping it up and down that mountain every Friday night, every time I went to the mall, every time I wanted to get a cup of coffee that didn't have a fast food logo on the side and I knew myself better than that.

Still, there were times when I just didn't have it in me to go back home after the day and so I'd shut myself in my office and curl up on a futon mattress I had folded up between two filing cabinets and I'd sleep on an airplane pillow with an old quilt over me. On those mornings I woke up there, I could just hoof it up to the gym early and catch a shower and change into spare clothes I kept in my office. I'd get breakfast in the cafeteria and enjoy the extra hour or so that would buy me.

My name is Jennifer McCordy. I'm a Big Iron system administrator – mainframe computers, old table-sized boxes that can do the heavy lifting for a large organization's back-end computing. I majored in Comp Sci as an undergraduate and thought I would just renew my lease and glide right into their graduate program but no such luck. They turned me down. Well, to be precise I got wait-listed, which is as good as getting turned down.

My backup was UNC-Asheville, so that's where I went. It beat spending a year slinging ice cream with my fingers crossed. Asheville had great big mainframes, old VAX systems no one else was running. I did my dissertation on the modern workforce's inability to cope with older technologies. That's what Y2K was all about: old COBOL programmers got called out of retirement left and right because they were the only ones around who knew how to fix all the old systems sitting around in aging coal plants and places like that. All the newly minted doctoral candidates in the world couldn't have solved that problem; it took a bunch of Santa Claus lookalikes in matching plaid suspenders to put the kibosh on the fall of western civilization. My UNCA profs loved it. I might as well have written them a three-hundred-page love letter. That wasn't what I meant to do, I wasn't angling for the sycophant's diploma, but it didn't hurt.

After that, even though Tim encouraged me to go get my PhD and become a professor – how many women like you, he'd ask, had no good role models in the sciences, in math, in computer science especially, and I agreed but I was also pretty tired of school by then. I decided to go get some live-fire experience. I figured it could only help my chances at getting into a good doctoral program if I had a few years of real system administration under my belt, something done out in the real world. So I started casting around for Big Iron jobs in Asheville because I'd really grown to love that slice of mountain paradise. I thought I'd have an advantage there, in fact, because of the lack of a high-tech industrial base. Asheville's economy is tourism and a few manufacturing plants slowly draining away to somewhere else. Landing a job nurturing some computer the size of a Cadillac and older than I was would be a piece of cake.

The only real nibble I got, it turned out, was from Mt. Ares Baptist College. They didn't have a computer science program but they did have a few old IBMs in their machine room, under the math building. Tim rolled his eyes. "They're never going to respect you at a place with 'Baptist' in the name," he said. "They're probably going to give you the hairy eyeball for not walking two paces behind any men who happen to be around." He called it Mt. Ares Burka College.

I don't want to give you the wrong impression about Tim. He's a good guy. I guess I love him, but to be honest I wouldn't throw myself off any bridges if he died tomorrow. That's not how I'm wired. He's followed me around from one academic program to another, though, and he never criticized what I was doing. He just seemed to want me to be happy and you don't find that every day. I took the job, and he never said another bad word about the place. I'd made up my mind and he respected that. Discussion over. Tim's that way. If he doesn't like something he'll say so and when he figures out that didn't convince you he'll shut the hell up.

When I took the job at Mt. Ares it was August. The last admin had retired in May. The systems they had going up there could basically run on auto-pilot for weeks at a time, no problem. They were Cold War-era systems that had been designed to keep the numbers crunched even if the Reds dropped the big one right on Washington. There was a real sense of that up in Mt. Ares, that idea that they were continually holding the line against some outsider culture determined to stamp them out. They hadn't replaced the systems they had, even though they could afford to, because they'd "always worked just fine," and I found out later they'd hired me in part because of my dissertation: *Legacy High-Performance Computing and Media Survivability.*

My first day was the week before the fall session began and my boss, J. Harley Boquet – I kid you not – showed me down to my new digs. His title was Dean of Information Management. What that means is that he was an accountant from the '60s. He attended Mt. Ares just in time to watch flower power bloom on television and I guess it scared him: he never left. He hired on that summer as a bookkeeper in the Finance Department instead and climbed the ladder one decade at a time. He had a habit of talking about his childhood home in Kentucky as though it were a Boy Scout camp that never ended. Maybe it was but I didn't really care. He's a nice guy, it's just, well, I'm not into standing around reminiscing. Anyway, he showed me down to my office. It was in the basement of the math building. We went down the front steps and cut around behind them and down another set of stairs; at the bottom of *those* there was a big double door, wooden, over-sized, big enough to drive a VW van through, with a huge sign on each so you could read the message even if one of the doors were propped open: NON-ACADEMIC.

Beyond them there was a hallway of plain, institutional puke green cinder blocks and a beige tile floor, the kind flecked with darker spots so you won't notice if it gets dirty. There were no doors along the first half of the hall, creating a sense we were moving deeper than we were, deep into the bowels of the building, out of the campus you'd find represented on a visitor map and into some secret, cavernous complex beyond that. For all I knew, we were. There were weathered, faded, metallic signs here and there down there with the standard radiation symbol and FALLOUT SHELTER written on them in block letters. After a few yards or maybe miles of green cinder block there was a double window, the right hand pane of which slid back so you could speak to an attendant on the other side. There wasn't an attendant anymore, but there used to be back when that was where the printer lived. Note the singular there: *the* printer. The glass was double thickness with a wire mesh embedded in it. I didn't know who they thought would rob this place, but it was bullet-proof all the same.

Finally, past that and around the corner, there were the double doors into the machine room. There was a big, red HIGH VOLTAGE sign with little cartoon lightning bolts all around it and a stick figure guy dying horribly in each corner. Fun.

J. Harley showed me the punch code – 1 2 3 4, I regret to inform you – and walked me back between a potpourri of different models of mainframes and data banks like mismatched LEGO bricks stacked in neat rows. In the back corner was a little door with no window and, in there, a small room with two filing cabinets, a plain wooden desk, a chair and no external view. It had fluorescent lights and all the charm of a converted closet because that's what it was.

Harley swept his arm inside and said, "Your new home away from home. I know it's not much but there's a powder room at the other end of the hall. Not a lot of competition down here for access to the Ladies'." Then he laughed his snorty little laugh, said he'd ordered a new nameplate and a desktop computer would be delivered next week and walked away. J. Harley doesn't know a lot about computers and didn't like that they'd brought in an outsider. If J. Harley had gotten his way, they'd have retained a portion of every class as breeding stock and then eventually they'd staff the place with a bunch of gilled natives of Innsmouth.

I spent the next week looking over the old wiring diagrams, such as they were, and figuring out where the hell everything was. My computer arrived a week after he'd said it would, but I had plenty to keep me busy in the meantime. J. Harley was barely speaking to me and no one else in the department seemed to know how to talk to a woman so I didn't make a lot of new friends. I used that time to poke around campus a little, check out the lay of the land and make a friend somewhere else: Everett Plank, Associate Professor of Biology. He called himself Underchair for Creation Science when he was feeling bitter about his job, but that wasn't often. I liked Everett. Everett was a good guy. We spent the academic year buddying around campus. I think Tim was jealous at first but then they met and even *Tim's* gaydar couldn't fail to pick up the beacon in the night that is Everett when he broadcasts the inner queen.

That first year at Mt. Ares wasn't easy. There were staff members who found me lacking in any number of ways: too female, too young, too non-academic. J. Harley turned out to be a nice enough boss, if a little weird sometimes, once he got used to having me around. He had an odd sense of humor and these horn-rimmed glasses that were so thick they made it actually impossible to look him in the eyes. He would tell jokes about Communists and Everett would say they were coded anti-Semitic remarks and I'd think to myself that they'd both been there so long they'd gotten decoupled from the rest of the world. Everett at least went down to Asheville to go dancing sometimes.

He made it a lot easier on me, though, while I adjusted. We had lunch together most days and sometimes dinner, too. The school cafeteria was uninspired to say the least but I'd rather have bland casserole with someone who makes me laugh than three lonely squares in isolation.

The Mary Anne McCollough Memorial Cafeteria was a dreadfully typical school cafeteria, exactly how you picture it even though I haven't mentioned the drab brown carpet an ascetic sixteenth of an inch in thickness, the iceberg lettuce on the salad bar, the malevolent main courses or the cashiers who sighed heavily whenever someone tried to pay with something other than an easy swipe of their meal card. The food was unbelievably bad, embarrassingly bad, and one time I realized as I was reaching for it that the "bread pudding" was made out of disemboweled Twinkies. Like, someone in that kitchen thought that was <u>okay</u>. The Mack was where nutrition went to die.

The one nod to luxury or the modern era in the cafeteria was the bank of TVs in the corners, three each. One was always on the Weather Channel, one was always on ESPN and one was always on Fox News. Sometimes someone would get a couple of friends and try to form a human pyramid to change the channels only to have a cashier come squalling out at them and chase them off before they succeeded. Everett would stare at the middle one, Fox News, and sigh every four minutes; then he'd joke that Bill O'Reilly was the best diet he'd tried yet as he pushed his plate away and draped a napkin across it.

"Why do you do that?" I asked the first time he did it.

"Dead food," he intoned, very seriously, "Is gross."

I survived a genuinely cold winter but we got less ice and snow than I'd ever seen south of the Mason-Dixon. There's an unmarked line somewhere in the mountains, west of which it gets *cold*. The month of April rolled around in due time and the ground started to thaw. Kids went on spring break trips and came back rowdy and paying zero attention in classes. Professors grumbled about kids these days. Adjunct faculty picked up their mail and scurried off with it in case they'd gotten a better offer. The tenured types started putting the tops down on their convertible K cars. Everyone was bustling. Seniors who were about to graduate started spending a lot of time just looking at things - trees, shrubs, the sides of buildings - like they'd never seen them before. April on a college campus is like that: something big is about to happen. Something momentous.

Everett and I were in the Mack getting dinner around the middle of the month when we both cracked up at something he'd said about his boss, Dr.

Bach, I don't remember what, and I realized abruptly that we were too loud for the ambient noise in the cafeteria. We were having a big laugh and everyone else was quiet. We looked around the room and what I realized was that everyone was doing two things: keeping quiet and facing away from us. I followed the directions they were all facing: they were all staring at the TVs.

"Again, this is a developing situation on the ground in North Carolina but we can provide some early details: there have been wide-ranging reports of attacks tonight by bands of wandering people. The offenders have been described a number of ways. 'Vagrants,' 'demented,' 'junkies'; these are all words we're hearing used on police scanners and in the reports we're picking up online and from some calls some of our affiliates in that state have received from local viewers."

There was a talking head, a news reader, sitting there looking thoughtful in split-screen opposite a guy in desert fatigues standing on the incongruously green lawn in front of a Fox station in Greensboro. "So, are you saying these are mass attacks? Would you call them riots?"

"Well, John, I don't know, but that seems to fit with what we're hearing, yes."

"Is this terrorism-related? Do you think this is terrorist activity?"

"Again, John, I just don't know that yet but it certainly could be. If so, they are extremely well-organized and they've recruited far more combatants than I would have thought possible."

"Can you describe them to us? The words you said people have been using, words like 'vagrant,' those strike a pretty strong chord. Are we talking about attackers dressed in rags? Are we talking about violent hobos?"

"Well, I..." The guy in the fatigues put his finger to his ear for a moment and then said, "John, we're piping you some footage just received by our local affiliate. The report I'm being given indicates that this was taken by a young police officer in the town of Hickory. The video comes from this brave young man's cellular phone. This is about to be shown for the first time."

The split screen faded and a blurry, pixelated image taken in too much darkness filled in the screen. It sat in freeze-frame for a moment and then, frame by trickling frame, the blobs moved.

They were people, marching. They were out of step and many were limping or dragging a foot and they didn't hold their arms out in front of them and none of them moaned or groaned or said anything you'd expect but they advanced painfully slowly towards the cop, the camera. He called out to them, hard to understand but closed-captioning claimed he'd told them to stop and raise their hands. They didn't. Something sparked and buzzed and hissed and I realized that he'd tried to taser the one in front but he'd missed.

Its face was hard to make out with the poor picture quality but something - a ridiculously cliché trickle down my back - told me I didn't mind not being able to make out the face.

The cop pulled a gun and shot. The person – *it* – staggered again. He fired at it again. It staggered again and it made a sound like a wheeze that was somehow much, much worse than moaning. The cop got his wits back, suddenly, and shot the thing in the kneecaps from maybe eight feet away. It toppled over and started dragging itself around on its elbows. The camera perspective swung wildly as the cop jumped back in his car, tossed the phone aside so that we got a great image of the roof of the Crown Vic, and then trees and street lights blurred by out the window.

I surprised myself when my first thought was confusion as to why they were described as vagrants; they'd all been wearing suits and ties or nice dresses.

The screen went dark again and then the two guys from Fox were on again. "That... is some very impressive footage."

"Agreed, John. The reports we're getting do indicate that's a fairly typical representation of what's going on. From what we're hearing, they've been spotted in a handful of relatively major population centers in the western and central portions of the state, with at least one report from the coast. We won't hesitate to let you know as soon as we have any further information at all." I took some issue with describing Hickory as a major population center but I kept it to myself.

"Any advice for viewers in North Carolina? Have the authorities made any statements or recommendations?"

"Only to say to stay inside, to stay with people rather than alone and to check before going anywhere that you have a stocked emergency kit including any prescription medications you might need. They've said to avoid travel even if you haven't seen one of these attackers because, and I quote, 'wherever you are, they could get there at any time'."

The talking head turned back to the camera and started summarizing for anyone who'd just tuned in. Then he ran the footage again. Still no one in the cafeteria spoke. We all sat in silence and watched the footage three, maybe four times in a row.

The news ticker on the bottom of the screen started to show what hashtags were being seen on Twitter: #NCattacks and #NCterror but nothing referring to the attackers themselves.

People started to trickle out by that point. No one who'd come in since it started had bothered to get food. The cashiers weren't at their stations, they were watching TV with the rest of us. Everett and I turned back to one another and he cleared his throat. "Call Tim," he said. "Make sure he's OK."

I nodded and dug around in my backpack and came out with my shitty little free phone for my shitty little first-year-staffer affordable plan. I called him and it rang three times before he picked up. "I'm driving up there," he said, a little breathless. "I shouldn't be talking and driving. The road..."

He trailed off. I still hadn't said anything.

"They're on the roads," he said. His voice was tight.

"Be careful. Come to my office."

I hung up and looked at Everett. "He's on his way."

He nodded and drained the last of his glass of iced tea. "Come on," he said. "Call him back and tell him not to go to your office. My office is nicer."

Everett and I crossed campus not quite at a run. We would walk really fast and then jog a couple of steps between the wells of lamp light here and there where a light had gone out, then walk really fast again. There were students out on campus who clearly had no idea anything weird was going on anywhere in the world but inevitably someone else would run by and, in so doing, pause to tell them some garbled version of what was at that point obvious. We had gone up the sidewalk at the side of the squat, brick Carl E. Hammerhead Student Life Center and cut between it and the more neoclassical, grey stone Joseph N. White Undergraduate Library and across the 1946 War Memorial Lawn - which everyone called the main quad - and then down between the Henry J. Swift Biological Sciences Building and the math department - the building where I worked - as yet unnamed because no one from any of Mt. Ares' math programs was both rich and dead.

Everett badged us into the bio department at the side door. We stopped at the bottom of that tall, winding stairwell with the carved and tooled hand railing and the clashing grey-brown tile floor and black tread strips on the steps. I didn't know why Everett had stopped until I realized - at the same time he made the same realization about me - we had both stopped to listen for shuffling feet. Neither of us had spoken on the way over and that didn't change now that we were indoors. I went up the stairs face-first, he followed three steps behind me, half turned to watch behind us. Halfway to the fourth floor, where his office was, it occurred to me that we were kind of stupid to come to the biology department. I mean, we've all seen the movies. There were probably labs full of reanimated frogs pissed as all hell to find out they'd been packaged for dissection.

At the door to the fourth floor I peeked through the small window that looked onto the hall and didn't see anyone or anything. Everett nodded and I yanked the door open, staying behind it, while he leapt through and spun around to check the walls on either side.

"Clear!" he said like he was a cop in an action movie, and for some reason that did it. I started to crack up. A snort escaped me. I clamped a hand over my mouth as I fought a wicked case of giggles. Then he made a breathy, adrenaline-poisoned sort of guffawing noise and four seconds later we were both laying on the floor laughing our fool heads off. I tried to gasp the word "clear" back at him a couple of times but I couldn't get out more than "Cl... cl...!" before I'd have to roll onto my side and curl into a ball and laugh until I was coughing and felt like I'd puke.

Two minutes later we were wheezing and panting and helping each other up and Everett had his keys in his hand. "Okay," he managed, "Let's have a drink."

I startled at that and wiped my eyes between blinks at him.

"I keep a little something around, yes," he whispered, "And no damned zombies are going to stop me from having one when I need it this bad."

I laughed again, quieter but still hysterical, a couple of surprised chuckles. I'd been in Everett's office a million times and I knew he hated the pomp and piety of Dr. Bach, the unspoken expectation that evolution would most definitely *not* be featured on any graded material in a given semester, all that, but I hadn't thought Everett would actually drink at work. In some respects, it's different for techs. It's so directly the opposite of what we would do. Well, the good ones, anyway.

We do *acid*. Everyone knows that.

He opened his office door and turned on the desk lamp as he walked around familiar corners in the dark. I waited for the light and slid into one of his visitors' chairs while he quickly and efficiently opened the bottom drawer of a filing cabinet, shifted a couple of overstuffed folders and came out with a bottle of scotch and a glass. The bottle was mostly full, at least, so maybe it wasn't so bad to have a tipple.

I caught my breath as I watched him pour. I'd started to think like these people. Christ, I hadn't even noticed, but it had seeped in somehow. That's the danger in a place like this. A prevailing attitude that everything is forbidden except what *you* like is easy to acquire. It's practically infectious.

Everett held the glass out to me with a pretty generous pour in it and said, "Cut crystal for the guests. I'll make do with a Dixie Cup." He stepped into the hallway for a minute and came back with a few big, red, disposable cups he'd snagged from the lounge down the hall or somewhere. I waited while he poured his drink, we touched our glass and cup together in silence and then we each downed what we had in a single go.

"How long before Tim gets here?" Everett was looking out the window, between the blinds, like we were being followed.

"He didn't say where he was." It was the first sensible, together thing I'd said since we'd been in the cafeteria and that felt like about six hours ago despite being about fifteen minutes. I coughed suddenly and then pointed at the window. "You know what that glass is?"

"What?"

"It's *clear*. Ha." I expected it to crack us up but it didn't. Everett kept looking out for a few seconds and I sat in silence, my face still hot from the run up the stairs and the laughing and the fear. Everett turned around, finally, and winked at me. It reset something about the tension in the air and I breathed again.

"So what do we do when he gets here?"

I ran my fingers through my long, sort of bland, sort of wavy but not really but still somehow kind of frizzy and sort of brown-black hair and pulled it back and half-heartedly tried to twist it out of the way while I pondered a response. "You have a TV?"

"Why?"

"We could keep an eye on the news."

"Oh they're just going to keep showing that stupid cop's cell phone thing," he said. "Or something like it."

I shrugged. Sometimes Everett could be a bitch when he'd had enough to drink. I really didn't want this one drink - okay, two - to be the start of a downhill slide into cynicism in a situation where we really didn't need cynicism. I resolved to do two things and immediately did them:

First, I announced that I needed to go to the bathroom, and did so. That gave me a couple of minutes in front of a mirror, kind of checking myself out. No wounds, no scratches, no bruises, no anything. That was good, to look at myself and see myself whole while my brain bubbled trying to understand, incorporate and include in my concept of the world exactly what seemed to be going on out there.

Second, on returning to Everett's office, I sat down and said, "You used the 'z' word."

Everett had the bottle within reach but he hadn't lifted it to his cup again. He took his eyes off it and smiled. "Well, you know."

"Know what?"

"Well, that's just good shorthand. It looked more accurate than 'vagrant,' you must admit."

"It isn't just shorthand." I kept my voice steady. "We both saw what was trying to come after that cop. He tasered it twice and shot it, what, five or six times after that?" I figured Everett was also remembering that moment when the thing fell down and started crawling forward on its elbows and that he was just as completely wigged out as I was. "That's not normal."

64

My phone rang abruptly, making both of us jump. It was Tim. He'd pulled up into the parking lot downstairs. Everett took the stairs down to let him in and they rode back up in the elevator. Neither of us said anything but it was pretty clear he'd come back up that route just to make sure there was nothing in the elevator already.

Tim and I hugged, gave each other a long kiss, hugged again. If you've ever been in that sort of situation, and had the chance to do that, you know why they do it in every movie ever made. Then the three of us sat in mostly silence. Tim didn't or wouldn't say much about the drive up from Asheville except to say that there were sections of the highway that were almost impassible due to wrecks or people simply abandoning their cars but that he made it. "I made it," he said. That was all the detail he would offer.

Everett went back to his window-staring and then we heard static in the air as an intercom system crackled to life. "The Biology Department has an *intercom*?" I looked sort of astonished. What was this, 1957?

"No," Everett said as he turned around and sat back down in his seat. "The whole campus does."

All students are requested to return to their dormitories until further notice. The voice was Chancellor Thomas. *All faculty and staff, the student government and all Resident Assistants are to report to the main auditorium of the Carl E. Hammerhead Student Life Center in thirty minutes. It is recommended that you walk in groups.*

It repeated twice more, with pauses of thirty seconds between the announcements. Everett and Tim and I sat together in silence and listened each time. Finally we heard the static whine of the intercom system turn off and Everett looked at Tim.

"Did you see any on the way here?"

Tim looked at him and blinked a couple of times, then nodded. "A few."

"How far away?"

"About... only about ten minutes outside of Asheville."

"There are a lot of miles of highway between here and there," Everett said after some thought. "We've got a lot of time."

"Were they—" I paused and swallowed air. "Were they headed this way?"

Tim kind of shrugged at me. "They were just, you know, there. They weren't headed anywhere in particular. I... I ran a couple over. It was an accident. They looked really, really - " but his voice caught, and he stopped and turned white.

Everett nodded at me and said, "We'd better go to the student center. We've got thirty minutes, though, so I suggest we take the time to arm ourselves."

"With what?"

"Mop handles, tire irons, whatever looks useful and doesn't require reloading."

I nodded at that and he and I left Tim sitting there in his office while we ransacked the janitor's closet on that floor. A little duct tape around the middle of a mop handle gave me something kind of like a staff that I could get a good grip on in a hurry, and Everett tried to show me a couple of moves with it in two minutes. Turns out he's a black belt in something. I don't know what. It has a complicated name. He said Jet Li knows the same stuff and then waggled his eyebrows a little. Everett has a thing for Jet Li.

I carried my mop handle and Everett carried two lengths of chain with padlocks on the ends and some yellow plastic tape that said CAUTION - CAUTION - DO NOT CROSS - CAUTION - CAUTION - DO NOT CROSS on a roll. I didn't even bother asking. We gave Tim a fire extinguisher that had some heft to it but he carried it hugged in both arms so that he wouldn't be able to use it to club anything that wasn't already ramming its head against his chest. He hadn't gotten his color back from when he went pale just *starting* to talk about the drive. I didn't push it.

The three of us left the bio building through the side entrance we'd used to come in and set off together towards the student center with fifteen minutes to spare.

I'll spare you most of Chancellor Thomas's speech. It was hurried and stumbling and basically he recapped the most sensational crap from Fox News. Then he introduced Security Officer Jacobs. Jacobs is a stereotypical donut muncher with a jarhead buzzcut. He was in Vietnam. He likes to talk about Vietnam, anyway. The truth is that anyone who was there, in my experience, doesn't so much like to talk about it. He's a retired sheriff's deputy who mostly rides around campus in a golf cart with a little blue light on top of it like the Grand Marshall of a K-Mart parade. He kept kneading his hands with one another while he spoke, rubbing the palm and back of one hand between the fingers and thumb of the other, then switching, while he talked. He fidgeted a lot. There was a taser in a holster on his right hip and when he wasn't kneading his hands into dough he would rest his right hand on it and put his left thumb and middle finger together and gesture with them.

"In light of the current situation," he said, thumb and middle finger hooked in an 'o' on his left hand and bouncing in rhythm to his syllables, "I think we should organize some safety patrols. No group smaller than three. Faculty would be matched with faculty, staff with staff. Resident Assistants should organize posted watches at any entrance to their dormitories and keep their residents inside. Cell service is functioning for now, so we can use that to keep in touch."

There was some murmuring in the crowd. "Is cell service expected *not* to work at some point?" came a voice from somewhere in the middle of the room.

Jacobs' forehead was sweating hard and his face was a deep red. "Well, I don't want to leap to any conclusions," he tried to say, but the next questions were already coming out: what about families of faculty members? Would anyone have to patrol with anyone else outside their department? Did they have walkie-talkies in case phones stopped working? How long until the power went out? Had anyone talked to the Sheriff's Department? Had one of the... *things* on the news been seen in town yet?

Jacobs did his best to shout them down, then: "I've called over to the Sheriff's substation on the Asheville Highway and got forwarded automatically over to the 911 center in Asheville. It..." He paused and cleared his throat. "It went to a message telling me they had an unusually high call volume." With each of the last six words his voice got more and more quiet so that the wave of noise crashed over the last two syllables of his response. He put his hands up and dusted off his nothing-to-see-here voice he kept in reserve for Homecoming games. "Listen... *LISTEN!* People, the Sheriff's Department has their hands full on the other end of the county. We are on our own here." He was booming, assertive, something we didn't often see in Jacobs. "We have got to keep our heads level and work together. I want to talk to Department chairs and hash out the details and then we'll give out orders from there."

Everett looked around the room, saw Dr. Bach in a pair of chinos and a button-up shirt rise and walk towards the front to join the other department chairs, then sighed and said to us, softly, "These crackers are going to get themselves killed. What say we form our own patrol team?"

Tim was pretty blank but I sighed and nodded at him. "You've got it." I wasn't relishing having to walk around with my mop handle and try to keep any math professors from getting eaten. We started to get up and try to sneak out but there was more bubbling up from the non-chair attendees so that someone finally got a microphone in his hand - someone I didn't immediately recognize - and pointedly said, "Officer Jacobs, exactly what are we facing out there? I've seen the news and they don't know what to call those people."

They're not people, came a few indistinct replies. One voice quite clearly followed that with, "They're Muslims!" I buried my face in my hands and tried not to scream. This was not what I needed to psyche me up for going on patrol to defend myself against the 'z' word. Someone else, a woman in a track suit, grabbed the microphone away from the guy who'd asked and turned her back on the stage to address the crowd.

"We all know what they are," she said, pointing out, away, wherever 'they' were. "They're the walking dead. We've all seen the movies. Jacobs isn't saying this but if we see one out there we've got to know what to do: we've got to kill them." There were a few open scoffs and jeers but there were a lot of silent, attentive faces that waited to see if she had anything else to say.

So, they *had* been watching the news.

Everett tugged on my sleeve and I took Tim's hand. We slunk out the back and ran almost head-first into J. Harley Boquest. He was standing there rubbing his coke-bottle lenses on a sleeve and glancing blindly out the big, double doors of glass at the entrance to the student center.

"Christ, Harley," Everett sighed. "You shouldn't be out wandering around by yourself." J. Harley wasn't all that fond of Everett on the grounds that Harley was universally intimidated by big, physically powerful black guys and it did nothing to help if they were, as he said it, "light in their loafers". This is the inherent contradiction of racism combined with homophobia: the black man is a terrifying aggressor, the gay man a nelly collection of offensive femininity, but a black gay man is somehow terrifying and weak all at once? I will never understand a mind that works that way. J. Harley Boquest gave Everett a look - having to look up at an almost 45 degree angle to look into Everett's very tall eyes, it's worth noting - that had any number of cuss words in it and then snuffled something half into his sleeve as he slipped the glasses back on. "Miss McCordy," he said to me as he tried to bounce past us and into the auditorium.

"Forget him," I said, though I wasn't sure to whom I'd said it. "Let's just go."

Tim, Everett and I set off back across the campus vaguely towards the biology department. "Can we just... hole up in your office?" Tim was speaking to Everett and Everett pondered in silence before answering.

"It would give us a view of the back of the biology department, at least," he finally said, "But that's pointed the wrong direction if these things are coming from Asheville."

"What about another office? Or a classroom?"

"No locks," I said. "Classrooms in that building don't have locks on the doors."

"A lab?"

Everett shook his head. "The labs are all in the basement."

We kept walking, naming buildings, finding them unsatisfactory. In time we were standing at the side entrance of the bio building, still having decided we didn't know of a good place to go and *hide*. Half the campus qualified as a bomb shelter in case of nuclear attack but nothing had been built to keep groups of people safe from ground troops. So, we turned and started walking again, diagonal to the way we'd come, and in so doing we started our own, unassigned patrol route.

Without discussing it, with no one really leading, we began a slow sweep of the outer edge of the main quad. At each point where a walkway branched off between buildings we would stop and advance slowly down it, checking behind shrubs and occasionally peeking into a dumpster or banging on its side to see if we scared anything.

We did two complete circuits of the main quad before we started seeing other patrollers. There were three faculty members from the Music Department, walking close to one another and wielding that long arm thing from a trombone. They stopped when they saw us, wary, but we waved at them, called out, and they eventually decided none of us were the walking dead.

I wish I could say the same about that kid who surprised them.

He was walking along with headphones on, hands in his pockets, his head down. They had just decided we weren't the enemy when they heard him behind them and spun around. One called out but he didn't hear them, didn't notice them, and then he looked up abruptly when he finally noticed them frozen in fear in front of him. He opened his mouth to say something and one of those music faculty simply swung the trombone arm thing around and clocked him with it on the side of the head as hard as he could.

The kid went down in a crumpled heap and twitched a little, so they hit him again, all three of them this time.

Tim made this muffled *grah* noise. Everett called out at them to stop and I ran towards them but by the time I got there it was too late. There was blood everywhere. A scalp wound bleeds a lot, way more than you'd imagine. The kid's pulse gave out four seconds after I put my hand to his neck. Nine o'clock at night and we'd had our first casualty from the zombie apocalypse before any of the zombies had even arrived.

The three music professors looked at me like I was crazy when I shouted at them to stop, that he wasn't one of *them*, that he just had headphones on, then turned and ran - just like that - in the direction they'd been going. I had to pull out my phone and try to call 911 to tell someone, Jacobs I guessed, that there was a dead kid laying in the middle of the quad but then I remembered what he said about 911 not working.

"Who do I call?" I said to Everett as he and Tim caught up. Tim was puking in a bush a few feet away. Everett was turning from dark brown to light brown, but he got it together enough to close the kid's eyes and kind of straighten his hoodie a little, fold his arms over his chest. "We didn't stick around to find out." My voice was strangled. "What number do we call?"

Everett scratched his neck and then walked over to one of the blue-domed emergency call boxes on campus. I heard him make a report to what sounded to me like a static line on the other end before he came back. "We'd better keep moving," he said, grave. "There's nothing we can do here."

I patted Tim on the back while he worked the last of it out of himself and then pulled out a napkin from somewhere in my backpack so he could wipe his face before the three of us kept going, a lot less certain of our route this time.

Going north past the student life center - now empty of the all-hands meeting from earlier - we started to run into other groups of three or four people on patrol. Most had a flashlight and nothing else. If you were in music or a janitor or knew how to break into the janitor's closet then you could arm yourself. Otherwise, you had a flashlight and a cell phone and not a lot else. They were all scared, all going very slowly, creeping along, nervous as cats and less capable. We learned fast that the way to be recognized as a human being was to speak quickly and clearly. If we did that right away, the moment they noticed us, they would eventually stop shaking long enough to say hello back.

Going farther north meant crossing Ares Mill Road and then wending our way along the parking lots and sidewalks that ran behind the five senior dorms that were as close to off-campus living as a town like Mt. Ares could manage. It was twenty after nine and we found casualties two through seven: kids who'd thrown themselves out of fourth floor windows.

Tim didn't have anything left in his stomach but that didn't stop him from trying. This time I joined him, one hand on his shoulder while I puked myself empty. Everett pointedly did not try to smooth anything over for anyone else who might find them. Fifty feet is a long way to fall. Pavement does some pretty nasty things to a body from that height. They had died afraid and their faces showed it.

We were walking away, a little more hurriedly, when we realized that there was singing coming from the open windows of the third floor student lounge in one of the buildings. It was gospel-y but very, very white. There was clapping that kept getting faster to rush the song forward. The singing sounded a little desperate.

"That's the Phreaks' floor," Everett said. This was apparently some subtlety of campus life that I had failed to pick up when hiding in my little closet-turned-office in the non-academic basement of The Math Building With No Name. I wrinkled up my brow at Everett and he started to smile a little. "The Jesus Phreaks," he said. I blinked at him, then kind of looked around us.

"You might not have noticed," I started, gesturing to indicate that maybe that was the whole fucking town, but he waved me silent with one hand.

"No, no, no, that's what they call themselves. They're a club: 'phreaks' with a 'ph' instead of an 'f'. They're kind of cheerleaders for God." He shrugged a little.

"Like, phone phreaks?"

Everett shrugged. "What's a phone freak?"

"A kid who hacks phone systems for free long distance. Old hacker hobby."

"That's silly," Everett smirked. "Long distance to Jesus is supposed to be free already. Haven't they heard?"

Tim stared up at the windows like... well, I don't know what the hell he thought would happen at those windows. Maybe he thought the Jesus Phreaks were working themselves up for a big mug of Sayonara Kool-Aid. That was certainly what it sounded like to me.

We kept going, hurrying a little, eager to get away from the dead and the cheerleaders for God.

Another thirty minutes of walking the outer periphery of campus - without bringing ourselves to wander into the town of Mt. Ares itself - took us by some freshman dorms, all silent, and finally the Mack. The doors to the cafeteria were locked at eight every night but someone had smashed in all the glass and then propped them open with a chair from inside. We could hear a lot of activity inside, some yelling, so the three of us advanced very slowly through the open doors and then the inner doors, which didn't lock, and then blinked back the bright light of the fully lit cafeteria.

In the middle of the part where everyone piles up trying to put their meal card back into their wallets and handle their tray at the same time, between the cash registers and the soda fountain, were three wheelbarrows mostly filled with food. A lot of it was just loose: hamburgers in shiny wrappers, little bags of fries piled on top of each other and a plastic bag that had been filled with the big, soft cookies from the ice cream bar. No one had been stupid enough to try to loot actual ice cream, so I guess the kids learn *something* here.

The hooting and chatter from back where people normally fill their tray started to die down and eventually an upper classman kind of swaggered - that's the only word for it - out from behind the cash registers with a baseball bat over his shoulder. He was young, white and muscular with close-cropped blond hair and a cleft chin that I'm sure charmed a certain type of young girl. "Oh, hey. Sorry." His voice was pitched exactly at that growing-into-manhood range between raspy and youthfully smooth. He set the end of the bat on the tile floor with an aluminum *tong* and kept his left hand around the butt end of the handle. "We saw three people walk in but didn't know if..." He smiled incongruously. "You know." He gestured at the wheelbarrows with his bat. "Want anything to eat? We figured we'd stock up now while the pickings are good.

"For how many people is all this food?" Everett spoke evenly but distinctly.

"Now, Professor Marsh..." The kid smiled and kind of cocked his head to one side, hooked the thumb of his free hand through a belt loop of his jeans and let his hand rest near his groin in a way that was weird. The vibe was very, very strange in the room all of a sudden. "We're not taking more than our fair share."

Everett's eyes didn't leave the kid's face. "Mr. Murphy, for how many persons is all this food?"

"The cafeteria has plenty back there in the freezers, you know. Delivery day was yesterday. They can feed everyone on campus three square meals for the next week at least." I kept staring at the kid's hand and I suddenly realized all this subtle or not-so-subtle body language was of flirtation. The hand near his crotch, the way he tightened and loosened his grip on the bat handle, the smile. I abruptly wondered if Everett had ever crossed that line, gotten involved with a student. It had to get lonely in a town like this. I had never really thought about it before. Everett's eyes still were on the kid's face, though.

"How. Many."

The kid shifted a little and all the flirtation fell away like fabric sliced in two. He was just an arrogant jock again, all of a sudden. "Well, there's fourteen of us on the team. Plus *girl*friends, of course." He smacked his lips in satisfaction after that. I couldn't read all the signals but I could see them being sent.

"Of course," Everett said evenly. "Take no more than is appropriate for the number. Take no more than enough for two days." He said this very firmly: "Be sparing in what you take. Remember that we may not have power for long. Eat the perishables first." Everett looked for some reason like he could murder the kid where he stood, then turned for the door.

I turned to follow him and Tim eventually did so too but said, "Shouldn't we take some for ourselves?"

"No," Everett replied. "We can come back on our next trip. They'll be gone by then. I don't think it's a good idea for us to stick around and force a confrontation with the baseball team at the moment." His face was really grim and I finally found my voice.

"That kid..." I paused, cleared my throat. "Was he, uh, flirting? Then? With the hand and the belt loop and the... you know? Stuff?" I knew he was already, of course, but I was watching Everett for his reaction. He smiled stiffly.

"Young Mr. Murphy tried last year to have me fired on grounds of immoral behavior. There's an old clause in the university handbook. I think he was hoping he could stick his cock in my direction long enough to make me forget." The smile was very brittle. "I don't care that he used such obvious tricks in an attempt to win my favor temporarily – more disappointed, honestly. What bothers me is subtler than that. He knows he and his little friends are stealing. He hoped to charm me into failing to turn him in but the thing is, he doesn't realize our situation."

I nodded and felt the color drain out of my face. "That there is no one to turn him in to," I said. "That we really are on our own up here; that anyone who might care on a normal day is too busy trying to figure out where to put the bodies of kids who threw themselves out of windows."

Everett nodded. "Those young men basically run everything in student life, or could if they bothered. They know that but that's pretty much the limit of their understanding. It's the outer border of the world they inhabit all the time, emergency or no. They'll soon enough figure out the absolute vacuum of authority we could be facing and I'd just as soon not be in the room when they do."

Tim let out a long, slow whistle. "Ruing. I think *that's* what this feeling is."

74

We were twenty minutes farther into our patrol when we heard gunshots and froze in our steps. Tim backed up a couple of paces but Everett and I looked at one another and then took off jogging towards the shots. We came around the corner of the English Department building and found four students in camouflage. They were milling around the outer perimeter of a small clump of bodies, maybe half a dozen.

I recognized a couple of them as faculty from the English Department itself.

As we approached, one swung his rifle around at us and the three of us dove into some bushes a second before he fired.

"Stop shooting!" My voice was hoarse and ragged from sudden screaming. "We're patrollers! We're okay!"

There was some muffled barking of orders or argument or something and then another shot over our heads. Then we heard boots running away, into the woods behind the English Department, and they were gone.

I started counting very quietly up from one and when I got to thirty I stood up just enough to peek over the bushes. No one was around. I stood all the way up and waited for a gunshot but didn't hear one. I turned, slowly, to look back the way we'd come; still no gunshot. I stepped out onto the path.

Still no gunshot.

Everett and Tim and I walked to within thirty feet or so. "Do you think they shot them by mistake?" Tim's voice was shaky. It struck me suddenly - thunderously - that he was the only person I knew who'd already *seen* one of these things out there in the night, on his way here. And he was out here with us. I couldn't believe how brave that was.

"No," I said in reply. I pointed at one, then another. "Shot in the back. These were opportunistic killings."

"That would explain the pot shot they took when we called out."

"It might be," Tim managed, "That they shot a patrol by accident and then another patrol came running and they shot *them* to keep from being caught."

"That's a big leap," I said.

75

"It seems like a good enough possibility," Tim murmured, a little wounded, and I reached out and squeezed his upper arm.

"No, not that. You may be right. If you are right, those kids made the jump from manslaughter to murder one in, what, a minute? Thirty seconds? That's a big leap."

"They've been told to protect themselves." Everett's voice was quiet. "They weren't told *from what* or that there were any limits to that."

I shuddered and pulled my arms around myself, the mop handle banging clumsily against my shins as I did so, and then turned to walk back to the quad. "Come on," I said. "We have to stop just walking around. We have to see if anybody has a plan."

They followed me for lack of anything better to do.

By the time we'd made it back up to the main quad, away from the little side-quad where a bunch of the humanities buildings were, the zombies had arrived.

Here's the thing about the South: there are cemeteries everywhere. Mt. Ares was founded in the 1880's and it had a functioning campus graveyard for ninety years. The graveyard filled, it turned out, during Vietnam. It was kind of small but I guess at the time the college was founded, when the college was two buildings and the graveyard was like a million miles away, it must have seemed plenty big. The population explosion of the 20th century is something that really took everyone by surprise, or at least it seems like it did. Everything from the 19th century seems so small, so cramped, so packed together by our standards like everything they built was for them alone, but they thought they were building everything on an *enormous* scale by their own metrics. There's this film called *Man With a Movie Camera*. It's from the 1920's. A lot of it was shot in Odessa, in the Ukraine. There are these scenes of the streets and they're just huge and wide and there's nothing in them. The people in those scenes at that time must have looked on those streets and thought to themselves, *We will never fill these streets*. Now Odessa is famous for its traffic jams.

That's a little off-topic. Sorry. The next part is hard to talk about.

The graveyard had a lot of graves in it. I'm guessing whatever makes people into zombies doesn't work too well when there's not a lot left to work *with*, which is as much detail as I want to go into about it. My point is, there weren't a lot of zombies but there were a few and they were almost all in military uniforms and they were sort of wandering around on the corner of the quad closest to the graveyard. Maybe the lights had drawn them. For that matter, maybe the gunshots had gotten their attention. I pulled out my phone and I hit the number for J. Harley Boquest who was, at least, someone I knew had a phone and would answer it if I called.

He picked up on the third ring. "Ms. McCordy," he said, very formally.

"Listen, Harley. Where are you? I need some... help."

"I'm patrolling with Officer Jacobs and Dr. Bach." J. Harley Boquest sniffed a little at that. He was pleased with having drawn a department chair and the head of campus security as his patrolling buddies. "We've just made a terrible discovery behind the senior dormitories."

"The jumpers?"

"Why, yes," he said. "Don't tell me a lady has been burdened with seeing them. Are you nearby?"

"No, we saw them a while ago." I couldn't believe I was standing there having a conversation with him about some dead people on the other side of campus when there were walking-around dead people fifty yards away and vaguely headed this direction. Tim was gawping at them, his jaw working in silence, and Everett was giving me this look of, *OK, seal the deal! Tell them what's happening!* and making that keep-going spinning motion with his right index finger.

"Good lord, girl, why didn't you tell someone? This kind of thing is deadly to morale." J. Harley's biggest problem was, seriously, that I hadn't called someone and now people might see those dead kids and *feel bad*.

"BECAUSE THERE IS NO ONE TO FUCKING CALL," I shouted, directly into the phone, held a few inches from my mouth. "BECAUSE THERE ARE ZOMBIES ON THE MAIN FUCKING QUAD."

"Mother of God!" I heard the phone clatter against the pavement and J. Harley was quickly marshaling Dr. Bach and Officer Jacobs into action. I could hear him faintly. "They're here! They're on the main quad! Mother of God, they're here!" Then there were some running footsteps and I hung up the phone.

Everett took ten seconds to point out two things.

"Girlfriend," he said, just as patiently as he possibly could, "Number one, don't shout when there are zombies around."

I glanced over and saw that all ten or so of them had stopped and turned this direction and some of them were... well, they were *sniffing* the air.

"Number two, whoever J. Harley Boquest has with him is going to know about it and so is anyone in a hundred-foot radius because J. Harley Boquest, goddess bless his cross-eyed soul and his Paleolithic glasses prescription, is not a quiet or subtle man."

I drew a breath before replying. "Is that a kind of good thing/bad thing statement? Like, good job on the telling someone who will let everyone know but watch the volume in future?" I blinked a little. Right now I needed... I don't know. I needed to be able to teleport, that's what I fucking needed.

"No. I take this opportunity to point out the caliber of most of the campus' reaction to this event." Everett said it very sweetly, and then he and I grabbed Tim by either arm and took off running in the opposite direction from the zombies, towards the senior dorms, towards where J. Harley Boquest and Officer Jacobs and Dr. Bach were going to be coming from.

I glanced back, just once, and the zombies were walking - not running, just walking - the same direction we were. Everett did the same, and then he and I had Tim off the ground and we were practically flying, ourselves.

We met J. Harley and the big, round, chino-clad bear of a man that is Dr. Bach, and Officer Jacobs. They were huffing and panting and Jacobs looked like he might be about to stroke out right there in front of us but they were running anyway and all of a sudden I had a lot more respect for all three of them and I was ready, just maybe, to believe Officer Jacobs' stories about Vietnam.

We skidded to a stop, set Tim down on the ground and didn't let go to keep him from running farther ahead without us. The other three stopped for just a moment, hands on knees, wheezing for all the world, and Everett and I talked all over one another in a wild jumble but we managed to communicate that the zombies were back there, in the quad, on the corner towards the graveyard.

Why no one had stopped to think about that I didn't know. On the other hand, for all I knew, someone *had* and they were laying dead in the graveyard or somewhere between it and here and no one else had any idea.

What surprised us was when we saw a few dozen other people running after them. We saw the baseball team - the sports dorm is next to the end of the row of senior dorms - and we saw the Jesus Phreaks, every last one of them, running with Bibles held up and some of them running with their eyes closed, someone else driving them by tugging a sleeve, their hands up, praying while they ran. There were some of them still singing and they formed a pretty ragtag band of cheerleaders for God if you'll allow me a moment of honest assessment. There were the four guys in camo, who I guess figured they were already out and they had intended to hunt zombies and Everett was right, J. Harley had screamed his head off the whole way there so every dorm and class building and parked car for ten miles had heard the news that real, dead zombies were on the main quad.

All of them - a hundred or more - ran past us in a single, endless crush and one of the guys in camo looked right at me as he ran by and I swear he recognized us, knew we recognized them, but he kept running. Everett put out a hand as though he was going to grab the guy's arm but I grabbed his wrist and jerked it back and let them go. "Not now," I said. "Later."

Everett watched them go and grimaced but he didn't say anything. In all the current of humanity going the other direction, Tim had managed to lose his momentum so that he stopped and watched them with us.

"They're all going to die," he said, simply. "I saw it in Asheville. People would try to gang up and then they'd get wiped out."

I blinked at him. "What?"

"Their resolve breaks down pretty fast," he mumbled. "Right away, in fact."

I wondered if he'd been in one of those gangs, if his resolve had broken down when he'd seen one of them do whatever it is they were doing to the people they attacked, and if that's what had set him on the road here. I hadn't thought about that yet, why he'd come here, why he hadn't just stayed in his apartment and locked all the doors and windows and called and asked me to come to him instead. He lives on the third floor of his building. Surely he'd be safe there. These weren't exactly agile creatures from what very little I'd seen. They were meat Daleks.

79

The crowd finished running past us and Everett and Tim and I fell into step behind them. We weren't running but by now neither were they. They'd seen J. Harley and Bach and Jacobs stop and go around a corner and they'd slowed down to follow. In time, all hundred or so of us washed out onto the main quad at the opposite corner from the zombies and there they were, the dozen or so of them, milling around but somehow vaguely towards us. I saw them lift their heads here and there and do what seemed like it must be sniffing, like they were smelling the air for our scents, and then they would kind of twitch and set off towards us with more purpose.

Dr. Bach was holding up his flashlight, one of those big, black Mag-Lite things, like a club. Officer Jacobs was holding out a nightstick, wherever he'd gotten one of *those*, but in his left hand; his right had the taser in it. J. Harley Boquest was trying to hold the crowd of students back. The guys in camouflage had swung out to the flank of the crowd and were setting up to take shots. I didn't know how much ammo they had - or how much they'd used on half the faculty of the English Department, for that matter - but they were lining up shots as J. Harley was trying to get them to put their guns down. "You could hurt someone with those things," I heard him bawling at them. "Where in tarnation did you even get guns? This is a weapon-free campus!"

That's when the Jesus Phreaks started singing again, singing with all their hearts. Their president - Spiritual Leader, I think is what they called him later, which is about as fucked up as it gets - was this bright-faced young kid who looked like he'd stepped out of a JC Penney back-to-school circular. He was rosy-cheeked and he had this cute little sprawl of a haircut that made him look like he was fifteen instead of 21. He was wearing a flannel shirt tied around his waist and Chucks and his t-shirt had a picture of Jesus giving a big thumbs-up in a way that I felt was probably meant to be ironic but that this kid *did not understand*. All that is just to help set the scene because what I heard the kid say, as he tried to shout over the singing, was, if I heard him correctly, "C'mon, guys, we can show these lost souls the way to their rest!" Then he and the rest of the Jesus Phreaks started walking across the quad, towards the zombies, singing and clapping and doing pretty much everything short of open ululations.

Jacobs was shouting at them to get back, everyone else was staring wide-eyed at the zombies and J. Harley was now running back and forth in front of the guys in camouflage, trying to get them to put their guns down. The zombies and the Phreaks met head-on and Spiritual Leader had his throat torn out in one swipe, like someone pitting a cherry.

Everyone behind him stopped singing and started screaming.

The panic that ensued is a little jumbled and hard to describe. One of the kids in camo stood up and grabbed J. Harley to drag him out of the way as the other three fired into the crowd. The zombies were going haywire, Jesus Phreaks pounding on them or passing out or running around in every direction. I saw puffs of dust in the light of the sodium bulbs overhead as bullets hit the zombies. I saw sprays of blood as bullets hit kids or zombies bit them or whatever was happening out there. It took a few seconds, tops, and then the kids in camo were trying to reload but J. Harley was hitting them over the shoulders with a wooden stake he'd pulled out from a section of grass on the quad that had been reseeded and roped off to keep people from walking on it. The guys in camo were yowling and diving away from him, crouched still, guns falling out of their hands as he walloped them there at the corner where shoulder meets arm. Everett and Tim had run forward to try to grab students and shove them away from the melee that had broken out in the middle of the quad, the baseball team only too glad to run the hell away rather than stand around swinging at dead guys in dress uniforms. Jacobs was screaming his head off and Bach was still standing there in shock. I saw a zombie take him down with one strike and then turn on Jacobs but the security officer still had that taser in his hand and he set it off.

The zombie froze and jerked and twitched and then landed on the ground with smoke curling from its flesh. Jacobs stared and blinked at it and turned as though to use it on another one but that one was already there and Jacobs, too, went down in a torn heap.

I ran over and grabbed the little megaphone from Jacobs' belt - he hadn't had a free hand for it before - and held it up to my mouth as I ran back towards Everett and Tim and J. Harley Boquest, who had single-handedly chased away the kids in camo.

"*Everybody,*" I shouted through it, "*Get out of the quad. Run this way, right now, and keep going. NOW NOW NOW NOW NOW!*" Somehow, that got through to them and the students who were still there and still mobile were all at once running back the way they'd come, around the corner, out of sight, back towards their dorms and the far end of campus. The zombies were pretty casual through that, some of them making a weird hissing noise when their arms would close on empty air as an undergrad got ten feet for every one of theirs.

In the span of ten seconds, it was Everett, Tim, J. Harley, me and - quick count - eleven zombies. The zombies all turned to look at me.

"Harley," I said, voice relatively even. "Do you have your keys to the Math Department?"

"Yes," he wheezed. Something wasn't right in his voice, but he was still walking. "Yes, girl, yes."

"Get them out. We - the four of us - are about to run to my office. But I am going to scream my head off the whole way there. Have we all got that? We are not going to do anything but run straight to the front doors of the math building and we are going to go where I say we go and I am going to scream the whole way. Is that clear?"

Three heads nodded. I saw Everett smile. J. Harley started to say something but I pointed my finger right at his ancient face. "I am giving the orders. You are going to do what I say. I do not have time for 'surely a lady' bullshit right now."

J. Harley nodded.

"One," I said, "Two. Three."

I flicked the contact on the megaphone and I screamed as loud as I possibly could. I screamed the girl scream, the one Fay Wray uses when King Kong has her in his grip. I screamed the way Judith O'Dea did, the way Elsa Lanchester did, the way Gloria Stuart did. I opened up, down deep, and I thought of that poor, demented kid from the Jesus Phreaks, of Tim and whatever he'd seen in Asheville to make him come here. I screamed for Officer Jacobs and the English Department faculty and a kid who'd try to get Everett fired one year and been so scared and so desperate to horde food that he'd flirted with him the next. I screamed for fat old Dr. Bach who'd stood there in silent terror and

I screamed for the fact that I didn't just get into damned UNC Chapel Hill to do my masters in the first fucking place.

I screamed the scream of humanity afraid, and if there's one thing movies have taught me zombies must answer, it's that.

Eleven zombies turned as one and started coming after us and the four of us ran as hard and fast as we could to the front door of the math building. Harley was fishing around on his key ring and finally got the doors open and the other three started to pull me inside but I put up a hand to stop them.

"We have to make sure they follow me," I said. Tim and Harley started to protest but Everett nodded and squeezed my hand.

"Come on, Harley," he said, voice very calm. "We've got to unlock every door between here and Jennifer's office as fast as we can."

"Open the janitor's closet down there," I said as they started to go. "Plug the drain in the sink and fill every bucket you can find."

I stood there and watched the zombies march towards me. I only backed through the doors and around the front steps and down the others into the basement as long as they could see me. I could see them, and they could see me - or at least the two or three in the lead could see me. I wanted them not to have a chance to get distracted, to wander off, to see a shiny and go for it instead. I needed all of them to follow me, right now. I was quick going down the stairs into the basement but they were pretty good at handling stairs that went down because, you know, *gravity*. Most of them toppled over somewhere along the way but they dragged themselves just like the one in that cell phone video from the news. I kept my breathing steady, kept moving, backed along the hallway past the industrial green painted cinder blocks and the mesh window with the bulletproof glass to protect a clerk that had been eliminated from the payroll fifteen years before. I counted the zombies as they crawled and shambled towards me.

Eleven. I really had them all, as far as I could tell.

Every single one of them had its eyes on me, eyes set in hollow faces caved in and rotted long decades ago, and not a one of them made any sound. It was the first time I realized there really was something *in there* and whatever it was, whether it was *them* or something else, it knew what I was and it was *hungry*.

I backed up the little ramp into the machine room and then I eased down an aisle between two rows of Honeywell DPS 7's which, to be honest, are from the late '80s, not the '70s, but they looked like something out of the '70s all the same. I noted their Carolina Blue coloring with some irony.

The zombies shambled up the ramp and through the doors, past the HIGH VOLTAGE signs, as ignorant as babes.

Everett and Tim and Harley had been busy. They had some of the panels off the floor to slow down anything that wasn't that great with footing. The two zombies that were still walking upright toppled over as one foot or the other plunged into the raised flooring and wedged between pipes of coolant. Some got hung up behind those. Some advanced on elbows without any problems and when they were all in the rows between my babies, the precious Honeywell's and the old IBM 360s and the UNISYS and the once-upon-a-time top-of-the-line Cray, I hefted the janitor's bucket that had been filled and threw it from the middle of my chest, with both hands, so that it struck one of those DPS 7's - the panel had been pulled open by Everett or someone - and sparks flew everywhere.

Everett heaved another bucket of water and hit another bank of machines and the zombies caught in the surge of electrified water moaned for the first and only time. Every time I'd heard them before - on the news, out in the quad, they had hissed. In the hallway, like I said, they had been completely silent. Now they groaned like living things in terrible pain.

Tim handed me another bucket and I threw it. Fire shot out of one of the computers. Harley watched this in abject horror, frozen, so I took his bucket from his hands and threw it myself. More fire shot out and a cascade of sparks flew out of one of the first ones we'd hit. Smoke poured out of it. The sparks and the fire had set off some sort of a reaction so that a geyser of sparks flew out of three entire rows and the lights flickered abruptly and Everett shouted, "Where to now?"

I turned towards the door to my office but that was crazy and I realized it in a second. So I turned back around and the four of us ran towards that sliding window. I threw it open and clambered through, landing hard on the tile floor on the other side, then rolled out of the way so Tim could follow, then J. Harley with Everett shoving him from the other side, then Everett finally squeezing his massive shoulders through the window and kicking out so that the four of us were out of the machine room and all the zombies were in it.

"The Halon system," I panted. "It's going to go off and kill the fire."

"Disabled," Tim gasped. "Everett threw a switch or something."

Everett nodded at me. He had gotten my plan right away. There were still machines sparking out and bursting into flames in there and the zombies that hit the electricity were frying fast. Still, some were mobile, so I ran back to the janitor's closet and grabbed a hose that was attached to the sink. I dragged it back down the hall and it would just barely reach to the clerk's window. I jammed the window shut on it so that it held in place and then I ran back to the janitor's closet. One twist of the knobs turned on the water with shocking force. Seconds later, water shot out and started spraying onto the remaining big iron in that room. Everett had already gone up the hall in his rubber-soled shoes to slam the doors into the machine room shut.

We stood there and watched water spray into the room and more smoke billow out of more machines and then the lights flickered and went out and the four of us ran, in unison, for the exit.

By the time we were outside and on the quad, I was laughing. Everett started laughing. Tim stared at us and then started to laugh and cry all at the same time. J. Harley Boquest just stared at the building and wept.

We laughed and cried and screamed and whooped and J. Harley produced a pack of generic menthols and everyone had one and coughed and sagged with exhaustion as we watched fire appear in the first-story windows of the math building, then from there engulf the other two floors..

That took a few minutes, in which we stood back-to-back to see if any more zombies were out. There weren't. We all went to J. Harley's house and I was so incredibly exhausted that I had no trouble whatsoever going to sleep in the middle of his living room floor. The rest of them sat up listening to the police scanner, but they never heard a thing. I figured the world would still be there for us when I woke up in the morning and if it wasn't, well, I was too tired to give a damn.

The next day we learned that twenty zombies had been found and killed in and around Mt. Ares. The report said nine because it didn't include our eleven from the math department; twenty was the real total. The fire, it turned out, had spread to the biology department before it had been put out.

There was another all-hands meeting two days after that at the student center and the chancellor wrung his hands and knotted his fingers together and announced Dr. Jane Dell would be the interim chair of the Biology Department in light of Dr. Bach's tragic, heroic demise defending students from an advancing wave of "the enemy". No one would say the 'z' word anymore. I'd only said it a couple of times myself and already it felt stupid to use it. I knew what they were, yes, but it seemed ridiculous to use that word.

"That woman," Everett said, listening to the news about Dr. Dell. "She hates me. I'm going to have to find another job." He shook his head and crossed his arms. "You don't know. She just *hates* me." I tried to tell Everett that was crazy, besides, what was I going to do without him? But J. Harley Boquest relieved me of that concern by firing me.

"You destroyed every computer in the machine room," he said, not looking at me, when he called me to his office a week later. "There just isn't a damned thing for you to *do*." So I moved back to Chapel Hill with Tim and got a job at an ice cream shop and applied for the doctoral program at UNC. I got wait-listed. This time I'm sticking around to see if it pans out.

Everett keeps up with me on Facebook. He found a job at a little school in Nebraska. "If you think Mt. Ares is full of the walking dead," he wrote to me in his first message, "You should see *this* town."

EDIBLE INTERLUDE

PRE-PACKAGED
SNACK CAKE BREAD PUDDING

A Recipe for the Adventurous or the Doomed

- 1 dozen prepackaged snack cakes with a cream filling of any flavor
- 2 cans sweetened condensed milk (or 2 cups milk prepared from nonfat dry milk powder + four teaspoons sugar or other sweetener)
- 1 can fruit-based pie filling of any fruit or fruit combination (optional)
- 1 jar of light corn syrup (optional)

In the grotesque wastes of the after-time, fresh ingredients will be hard to come by; this recipe has the advantage of relying entirely on products that were prepared for human consumption long before humans become the consumed. To make this recipe, you will need one implement capable of cutting doughy snack cake material and scraping out its insides, one pan, one bowl and patience.

Open the snack cakes and slice each in half then scrape the creamy filling into the bowl. You should tear each emptied snack cake into shreds that are slightly smaller than bite-sized then place the pieces in the pan in a loose pile. Shake your cans of sweetened condensed milk (or milk and sugar) vigorously and mix in the corn syrup if available; pour the milk and/or syrup over the shredded snack cakes to drench them. Mold the resulting mush into a lumpy mass in the pan. You want it to be obvious that the pudding was once different types or units of pastry and stuck together. Open the canned fruit filling, if using, and use to coat the outside of the bready mound, then spread the creamy filling across the top to crown the affair. A traditional bread pudding would have been baked in an oven but that luxury is probably no longer available to you. If it is, you need merely warm the dish. Slice, serve and enjoy in a world that no longer has time for low-carb diets.

THE DOORBUSTERS

The second zombie apocalypse started on Thanksgiving, six years later, at the front door of an all-night ÜberBargains.

Technically it was two minutes after midnight on the day after Thanksgiving. I was just about smack dab at the head of a mob of people trying to get to a huge pile of cheap Blu-Ray players in the first minutes of Black Friday. "We" had been in line for two days, camped outside the store like refugees at a neutral border crossing. I have to say it like that, with the little air quotes and everything, because in truth I'd simply shown up the first night and done my vampire hoodoo thing to implant this suggestion: that when I showed back up at the last minute the people at the front of the line would remember I'd been there the whole time.

I brought them donuts and coffee that first night to say thanks. I even introduced myself as Withrow instead of using a pseudonym. I'm not a total animal.

I got to the store on Thanksgiving around 10:30 PM. I brought a big plate of biscuits I'd made and a tub of turkey I'd roasted and carved. I also brought Smiles with me, of course. He was wearing the red Service Animal vest I'd bought him off the Internet so nobody would object to his being there. It might be hard to imagine anyone openly objecting to a hundred fifty pounds of Doberman when it's right there in front of them, teeth and all, but people are nothing if not full of surprises. I'd had that idea of getting him a vest one night after someone at the movie theater tried to say he couldn't come inside with me because of health codes and other assorted forms of bullshit. Now whenever anyone looks like maybe they're pondering whether to point out how obviously not blind I am then I tell them I'm his trainer and I say, "He does really well with strangers who keep their distance. Mostly."

The biscuits and the turkey got passed around to all my hypnotically suggested pseudo-friends at the front of the line and they gobbled them right up. I tossed a couple slices of turkey at Smiles so he could catch them out of the air one at a time and consume them in one bite. My placeholders were only too happy to eat our grub and watch our antics. A body who shows up with free food and a clever dog can get through almost any door in the world.

What surprised me a little bit was the appearance in the parking lot, on one of the concrete islands between rows of parking spaces, of three tents and four slightly scruffy individuals, one of whom was holding a well-made handwritten sign reading REMIND ME OF THE REASON FOR THE SEASON and another whose placard read OCCUPY THANKSGIVING.

I wasn't so thoroughly out of the loop as to have no idea about the Occupy thing but I was pretty surprised to see them for a whole mess of reasons. When I pointed and opened my mouth, one of my temporary friends from line - an African-American woman named Jolie who was there to buy a TV for herself and a steam cleaner for her cat-hoarding mother - smiled and chuckled. "I love those kids," she said.

"I don't have any objection myself," I replied, "But I'm a little surprised the store hasn't run them off yet. Private property 'n all, you know."

Jolie shrugged. "Trespassing arrests in the parking lot don't put people in the shopping mood. They just got here around sundown. They're pretty smart about the timing." She tapped the side of her forehead with her index finger and winked.

The funny thing about Thanksgiving is that it's always been a feast day for vampires, too. You wouldn't think so maybe, what with so many mortals staying home or traveling to be with family and friends, loading up on tryptophan and then falling asleep in front of the Lions game, but that's probably because you're in the majority of people with somewhere to go and someone to see. The usual vampire haunts on any other night – the seedy bars, the dance clubs with dark corners, the alleys where the foolish or the unwary try to take shortcuts – may see reduced traffic on a night like Thanksgiving but the traffic they see is immeasurably safer prey. Not to pass judgment, but the truth is some slob in silicone clogs in the parking lot of a Hooters on Thanksgiving night is going to take a while to be missed.

People disappear all the time – a million people are reported missing every year in America, and that's before we get to all the people termed "missing missing," the people who disappear but no one knows or cares because of the circumstances they were already in when they vanished – and even though the statistics don't actually support it, the stereotype is that they do so around the holidays more than any other time of the year. Bottom line, it's easy pickings for my kind and we are not universally the sorts to turn down an opportunity to get a little crazy once in a while.

All of that changed the last couple of years, though. Some of us liked to stay in, sure, and some of us didn't behave any differently than any other time and I don't want to give the impression of some artificial uniformity of mindset amongst us because we're as different from one another as any other class of person. My point is the trend towards earlier and earlier openings for the "day" after Thanksgiving sales have started drawing us in, too, here and there. We may be the things that go bump in the night but we like a bargain just as much as anyone and I'm certainly no exception. I'd gotten by on a VCR and a bunch of old VHS tapes – and some new ones I'd bought online because friend let me tell you, the Internet is a new technology that has extended the life of nearly every old technology – but I'd finally gotten talked into upgrading by my cousin Roderick.

Yes, vampires can have cousins, Southern ones especially so.

Roderick told me what to look for in a new TV and so I'd bought one of them online and set it up myself. The VCR looked like shit on it, though, and that's when he'd told me to go buy a Blu-Ray player. There was no deal online as good as the one I could get if I showed up for this sale and it had been months since I'd played tourist amongst the living so I'd said, hey, why not?

At ten minutes past eleven a couple of managers from the store came down the line asking each of us which of the big, limited-quantity deals we were there for and handing out these color-coded slips of paper as our "tickets" for each particular deal. I got handed a slip of green paper when I said I was there for the Blu-Ray thing and when I asked why they were using green instead of blue, with kind of a smart-ass smirk, the woman handing out the chits gave me a look that could have made a kettle freeze over mid-whistle. "Blu-Rays get green paper," she said. "Televisions get blue paper, vacuum cleaners get orange and comedians get a sore lip. Would you like yours now or later?" Then she smiled the sourest, sleepiest, most hateful smirk I'd seen on a mortal face in years. I loved it, and when I roared in laughter and everyone around me jumped she actually allowed herself to look sincerely amused for just a flicker of a second.

Her boss, I supposed, was standing in earshot and came chugging over with a look of panic on his face. "What did you just say?" He was a big fat fellow not that unlike myself but he had a squeaky little voice that made me want to put my fingers around his neck and squeeze it until he stopped making any noises at all: talking, breathing, whatever. He turned to me and lowered his voice to a breathy whistling whisper in hopes no one would overhear. "Sir, I just heard everything and I apologize for Jenny's behavior." He faced her again and squeaked, "You're fired! Immediately! Go, now!"

Before the woman could turn away or the man could say anything else I clapped a pudgy hand around one shoulder on each of them and looked deep into the boss' eyes. My voice had that little extra supernatural something behind it when I said, "Jenny said nothing to offend me. I am a happy customer. I intend to purchase more than originally planned because of our interaction." My gaze flicked around to Jenny's wide, surprised eyes. I could see what she was thinking, not through some exceptional psychic power but because I had seen that expression a hundred jillion times since 1977: *holy shit, Jedi mind trick.* Before anything could settle in I bored into her mind with my own and said, "Stay sassy, Jenny."

What surprised me was when her mind bounced back like it was covered in bubble wrap. She said, crystal clear and in no way hobbled or befuddled by my attempt to force my will onto hers, "My name is *Jennifer.*" She gave the nametag a disgusted flick. "But they already had one that said 'Jenny'." She looked from me to her boss, who bore the thousand-yard stare of someone whose brain is still processing new instructions, then back at me. "I'm not asking. I don't even want to know." She shook my hand off her shoulder, shoved a green scrap of construction paper at me and said, "Enjoy your shopping experience."

Just like that, she was going down the line again. Her boss snapped out of it five or six seconds later and then said, "Good work, Jen… ny?" She wasn't there but I was. I gave him a friendly grin. He returned it on autopilot and wandered off to collect himself. Smiles panted at his back in a friendly way.

I looked at Jennifer where she was progressing down the line and shuddered. A mortal who could resist the hoodoo was one to steer clear of or to remember in minute detail.

By quarter of midnight everyone in line had gotten a chit if there were one to be had. There were a bunch of people who left at that point, not having gotten there in time to have a serious chance at the thing they wanted, but there were forty or fifty of us who were absolutely going through those doors with our tickets to shop clutched in our respective fists. For that intervening half hour there was a woman a few yards back who talked continuously on her mobile phone, barely stopping to breathe, generating a near-constant stream of consciousness centered entirely on how she was going to get one of those goddamn "highly defined" televisions and how, and I do quote from memory, "Nobody had better get in her way because she was going to get one of them teevees if it killed her to get it she would hurt people if she had to because she had not set up shop in front of that store for two days just to have Hank not get his Christmas present I mean Jesus did not die on the cross so that people could have lousy Christmases isn't that what Christmas is about anyway but you know nobody wants to say Merry Christmas anymore it's just Happy Holidays and everyone knows Happy Holidays is Jewish for fuck you."

I kept balling up my right fist and then unclenching it again throughout her litany of stupid. I wanted to put that phone so far inside her the phone company would have to hire a surgeon but there was no such luck; not this close to cheap Blu-Ray o'clock, anyway. I'd already been riding the hoodoo-go-round pretty hard with this crowd and I decided waxing this one obnoxious twit and then trying one more mind trick on the whole gang might just be pushing my luck. Instead I bit the insides of my own cheeks every time she drew another breath. As you know, my hearing is very good and I realized abruptly that I had no idea what the person on the other end of the phone call sounded like and, in fact, hadn't heard *them* breathe in some time despite my ears having no problem with all the electronic distortion and intervening space between me, that woman and the other end of her telephonic connection. She was talking to a handset someone had set down and walked away from and she didn't know or didn't care. It probably happened all the time.

It didn't make me hate her any less but it did make me smile.

Enough people asked the manager how he would know it was midnight that he had to publicly declare that he would be using his cellular phone as the official clock and there was some grumbling because a few people preferred their own slightly fast-running watches and the like. He stuck to his guns and I said fairly loudly that it sounded reasonable, it wasn't like any of us had to rush home for dinner, and for some reason people processed that as a joke and a few of them even laughed at it despite it not being funny at all. Humans are weird animals. Any one of them might be Einstein but you get fifty people in one big herd and they turn into sheep or they turn into wolves and it's a toss-up which way they'll go every single time. Either way, no two people are as smart as any one and the curve seems to be geometric from there as the number increases.

At midnight most of the staff disappeared inside before the manager made something of a show of opening the doors and gesturing for us to enter. Those of us at the front tried to balance on the knife's edge between polite forward motion and running full-tilt for whatever precious thing we were there to obtain. I was content to mosey – we had tickets to shop, what was the point of rushing? – but that slag with the phone started trying to rush forward. She elbowed a little old lady on her way through the crowd and when Phone Lady got to me I couldn't resist the impulse to bite back in some fashion. I did an arms-out, wobbling double-step dancing pantomime of lost balance that I've used a hundred thousand times to trip up prey. The toe of my boot wound up on top of her ankle and it took the tiniest push to send her toppling over in a heap in the middle of the sidewalk. To be honest I'm not really sure why I did it other than reflexive annoyance at having to listen to her bullshit for an eternity beforehand. Later I tried to convince myself that I was doing it for everyone else, too, as secondhand revenge for all the people who no doubt loathed her to their very core after two days and nights of that constant yammering, but the truth was that it was all me. I didn't like her and so I tried to hurt her because sometimes that's what I do to people I don't like.

She went down screeching into her phone and then, very shortly, into nothing but air when the phone flew out of her hand on impact and skittered across the sidewalk in front of the store, between the feet of countless strangers and out onto the asphalt. The crowd behind her got a little tangled up and people bounced off one another. I kept moving, Smiles by my side, and didn't stop to turn around until I was completely through the doors on the basis that the last thing one should do when assaulting someone as I had just done was to make a big show of sticking around to see what happens. By the time I let myself look back Phone Lady was beetling – on her back, limbs waving, helpless – and shrieking at the top of her lungs. A young fellow behind her in line reached down and tried to take her hand to help her up but the woman was so lost to surprise or self-interest or the absence of her precious phone that she misunderstood and started screaming even louder:

"MASHER! MASHER! HELP!" She was hysterical and immediately started fighting back against the kid's attempt to assist. I wondered how long she'd been in line and whether she'd had anything decent to eat. Maybe she had forgotten to bring her meds with her. Maybe she was insane to begin with. Maybe there had never been anyone on the other end of that phone call in the first place. Some atrophied emotional muscle twitched in imitation of something I might on reflection have classified as guilt and I hesitated. I wondered if maybe I should go help her up. She was a lot less likely to break my arm than she seemed to be the kid's, who for his part was starting to look a little scared at the ferocity of her response to his act of goodwill.

I opened my mouth to say something across the gap of the double-doored airlock entrance when much to my and the kid's and everyone else's surprise the lady's other hand came up out of some pocket somewhere with an oversized spray can. It let out a sharp pop when her fingers scrabbled across the top of it and a cloud of something white and glittering exploded into the air around all of them but especially into the face of the kid, at whom she must have pointed it. Everything froze in place for half of a heartbeat before the kid's mouth opened and his eyes closed. Something – some sound - came out of him that sounded like strangled death. It was a scream and then it was a shriek and then it was… I don't even know what it was. It was a squeal shading into a whistle and then the air ran out but he looked like he was still trying, still digging around down there in his chest cavity for one last bit of breath to push out.

Smiles' ears twitched and he started to growl.

A few people standing around fell over coughing and a couple more, arms over their faces, ran around the splayed forms of the two surprise combatants and through the doors of the store. Store Employee Jennifer was standing by the door on the inside of the giant airlock. She was quick on her toes and had slammed a big red button on the wall, hidden from sight by one of the anti-shoplifting scanner things, so that the external and internal doors of the store slammed shut in a flash. With her other hand she produced a phone.

Something about the anguish on that kid's face held me transfixed. I don't enjoy needless suffering but something about that guy's pain was hypnotizing. He was just some kid of maybe twenty five years: skinny, Asian, crew cut, wearing one of those puffy winter jackets and girl jeans like the kids these days seem to prefer. He was cute and he'd wanted to help and now he looked like something was trying to turn him inside out. I think I was waiting to hear him scream again just so I'd know he'd drawn another breath but it kept not happening. Phone Lady was screaming too, caught in the cloud of her own making. I had to figure it was pepper spray or something, one that had malfunctioned, but the can was way too big to be pepper spray unless she bought it in bulk. That bad boy was economy size or nothing at all.

The can itself fell out of her hand and rolled towards us, banging off the outer front door of the store, and my eyes zeroed in on it. The label was in Russian, a language I thought it might be useful to study during the long decades of the Cold War. My spoken Russian is pretty much useless but I can read it very well. The label read in the dense text typical of Soviet military goods, "Self-defense caustic spray for deployment in crowd control scenarios. ATTENTION: DO NOT USE WITHOUT PROTECTIVE GEAR."

There was a date but it was in the old Soviet fashion, mixed into a coded string that included the lot number and the factory. The important part was the number in the middle, the year of manufacture, and it read 77. The lady had just tried to use a 35-year-old incapacitating aerosol grenade – common back in the day and it still is in certain situations – like a can of pepper spray. A part of me idly wondered whether it was maybe some outdated Kolokol-1 or a mix of MPK and tear gas or just straight pepper spray or what because the rest of me was still transfixed in horror as the skin on the lady and the kid visibly blistered. Christ Almighty, she'd deployed a chemical weapon. Smiles' growl had held steady and his whole body was poised to spring even though there were two doors and ten feet between them and us.

Jennifer snapped her phone shut with obvious annoyance and said to no one, "Stupid big-box stores. I can never get a signal in here." She tapped me on the shoulder. "Sir," she said, "Did you get sprayed? Are you OK?"

I blinked and tore my eyes away from that kid – he and the woman were still frozen in place in a rictus of agony, utterly unmoving – and shook my head. I cleared my throat to speak. "No, no, I'm fine." I paused, and then I remembered the polite thing to say. "Are you alright?"

She waved that off. "I'm fine. Just… I don't know, I guess go get whatever you came here to buy. Someone can ring you up while we call 911 and try to clear up all this idiocy." She gestured exhaustedly in the direction of the outside, the front of the store, and so she and I both looked out there again.

The kid and Phone Lady were both standing now, which was a relief for the half a second it took to process the looks on their faces: wide eyes, wider mouths and hands that clutched at nothing as their gaze jerked back and forth, wild and random and with a look that made me think of nothing so much as one night a few years ago at a meeting of my neighborhood association's executive board. I reflexively drew a short breath and then cut it off. I worked my jaw for a moment before saying, "Yeah. Shopping. I'll go do that." I looked sidelong at Jennifer and couldn't help but notice that she looked frightened, yes, but that her jaw had set with surprising certainty. "Yeah," she said, never looking at me, her voice as smooth as a steel beam. "You do that."

I turned away from her and from the doors and that horrifying sight outside, away from the memories of all those houses in my neighborhood where I'd gone and knocked and found them empty, away from the memories of the ones I'd found that were still dangerously occupied, and I ran directly towards the back of the store, past the big displays of television sets and BluRay players and off towards the two sections I thought might have something useful in this situation: sporting goods and garden tools. Smiles was never more than three feet away, his little cape flapping absurdly as he ran.

I went through Gardening first but ÜberBargains is more of a clothing and groceries and media place than it is a heavy duty hardware store. They didn't have anything that overwhelmingly exceeded the gifts my undead condition already gives me but I grabbed a garden fork with a shaft about a yard long and on my hurried walk through Kitchen Equipment I grabbed a long knife with a rubberized handle that, at a quick wobble, seemed relatively well balanced. When I arrived in Sporting Goods I went straight to the aisle labeled BASEBALL/SOFTBALL/TENNIS and there I found Jennifer holding a long softball bat out with both hands as though weighing it. She nearly jumped out of her skin when I came around the corner with my billowing old black trench coat and the glower of someone readying himself to do unpleasant work. Abruptly she recognized me. Her eyes narrowed in suspicion.

"Electronics are over there." She gestured easily with the bat. She'd carried one before, had swung one many times. Her gesture was effortless, thoughtless. "Aisle I-27."

I held up the garden fork and the knife. "I brought you these."

She arched one eyebrow at me. "Why?"

"Because we need to contain the threat." I said it in as matter of fact a manner as I could. I didn't want to sound hysterical and I didn't want anyone else who might overhear me to perk up at some unusual tone of voice.

She studied me carefully for three of her own heartbeats, then wobbled the bat in her hands. "I'm more comfortable with this, but thanks. How did you know where to find me?"

"Lucky guess."

She produced a little chuckle that was not amused. "And I'm the queen of Spain. Why don't you need them yourself?"

I hesitated, and she saw me hesitate, and she impressed the hell out of me by saying, "Later, when we're all okay. Right now we have zombies to kill."

When she said it – with the Z word and everything – that made it real. Everything snapped into focus too quickly and I held up a finger. It was partly to correct her but it was partly to give myself a second to reorient myself. "Not kill. Contain."

Her mind worked for a second, and then she looked me dead in the eye. "You brought piercing and slashing weapons. Those don't produce a lot of containment, generally speaking, and anyway we need weapons that do bludgeoning damage." A pause as she nodded at Smiles where he stood beside me, his back turned to us as he watched my back. "Luckily for him, the jaws of an animal do all three."

"Did you just make a *Dungeons & Dragons* joke?" I blinked at her in slow amazement. I'd gotten it, of course. One has to pass a lot of long nights when one plans to live forever.

"Don't change the subject." She was stern and I could hear in her voice that she did not relish this return to duty; this re-immersion in whatever specific experience had never quite ended. "And don't pretend we can just sit on those monsters and hope they get better, either."

"Sister, compassion isn't what's holding me back." I glanced towards the ceiling and the nearest of the omnipresent black half-spheres attached to it. "This place is covered up in cameras and I'm not interested in a murder rap."

She followed my gaze and turned down the corner of her mouth in obvious displeasure. Jennifer was serious, thoughtful, thinking tactically, but she hadn't worked out a strategy beyond Kill Everything. I'd seen a couple of vampires go on benders and have to be put down but those were episodes of chaos and opportunistic attacks made without any thought beyond getting at the nearest bag of warm blood they could find. Jennifer's expression and manner were almost reptilian in comparison: cold and calculating. "If this is what we think it is," she replied, "No one is going to blame us for what's about to happen. Hell, they'll hardly notice who actually does the 'save the day' part."

"I know now isn't the time to ask," I said, "But what do you do for a living? I mean, other than this. Did you used to be, like, a Marine or something?"

Jennifer snorted at me. "I'm a mainframe systems administrator." That was just word salad to me and my blank look said as much. She elaborated with great patience. "I'm an engineer."

I nodded. "Got it. You build stuff." The look on her face said I was wrong but I had other concerns. "Now back to figuring out how to disable instead of kill. I don't doubt I can hold one of them still and maybe you could, like, hit them upside the head or something, or tie them up. Last time I…" I cleared my throat. "Well, let's just say killing wasn't off the table. It was kind of the main course. It was different, though. They'd been dead a long time. We're smart enough to know the difference between them and this." I gestured vaguely in the direction of the front of the store. "These people are under the influence of a chemical weapon and there might be some way to help them. Even Smiles here knows the difference between disabling and killing, promise. We can do just as well or better. These are not *those*, or at least we can hope not."

Her eyelids relaxed and her gaze unfocused for a moment as the movie of her own history played out. "Mine had been dead a long time, too." She shook it off at the sound of a distant scream. "Let's go."

"Hell," I said, "They might not even get inside. They're outside. And you said you were going to call the cops. We just have to keep the lid on things for a few minutes, right? Get these under control, you call the cops from outside and bang, we're back to normal."

She looked at me with something I couldn't entirely parse but I saw in it a little fear and a little pity and a whole lot of sadness. "I said let's go."

We turned together and half-jogged all the way towards the distant front of the store, neck and neck and neck.

We had been gone from the front door maybe four minutes, five tops, and I figured the general front door area of the ÜberBargains would be a killing field or empty of any sign of life except for the handful of initial victims of whatever that lady had used to gas everyone. Instead, it was like a Laurel and Hardy routine in slow motion. Most of the people out there were still out there, though some had taken off and I noticed some empty spaces interspersed between the cars that were still there. Some people were just stupid, I guess, or determined to get their goddamned big-screen television, and some of them were obscenely fascinated by what was happening. I mean, it wasn't like the existence of zombies was a secret but not very many people had seen one.

Everyone saw it on the news when it happened and lots of people on the Internet claimed to have seen a zombie or even to have fought and killed one that night but the truth is that there was only a tiny handful of survivors who had seen any real action that night and it was easy to spot that they were telling the truth. When they would get interviewed on some thirty second anniversary spot on the local news, for instance, I could always tell if they were for real by their hollow gaze and the way they didn't seem too enthusiastic to talk about whatever experience they had to endure. It's kind of how I imagine it must have been to stand on the street and watch one of the planes hit on 9/11. Lots of people claim they were in New York or that they heard something in the distance but nobody much seems to get out there and brag about watching a few hundred people die in an instant. Footage of the crashes has a kind of sacrosanct quality, like a sixty frames per second tombstone, and for all that our collective half-invented memories of the events themselves are routinely exploited by politicians and media assholes and everyone else who makes a living listening to the sound of their own voice, no one seems eager to put the actual events on television to remind anyone of anything in particular. The drifting gaze and distant stare of an actual experiencer of Z Day are unmistakable and they do nothing to glamorize the event.

The people outside the ÜberBargains were mostly moving in big arcs and swoops, some jogging in place to try to stay ready to dodge, but mostly just doing whatever seemed to keep them away from the people who initially seemed to be affected: Phone Lady and Helpful Kid. They were advancing slowly, arms twitching, eyes rolled back in their heads, jaws slack, moving towards whoever screamed next. That person would basically lead them around the group while everyone else dodged out of the way until someone else screamed and the zombies' attention was drawn to them instead.

A couple of people were on cell phones and one of the other kids who had been out there was filming everything on his fancy phone. People are so stupid sometimes.

"Okay," I said, but so had Jennifer. We had both looked at one another to issue an order. We both paused. Then we both opened our mouths, stopped again and finally I said, as fast as I could, "You open the doors the next time one walks by and we'll rush them." I gestured at Smiles.

Jennifer looked away, at the two walkers, and then nodded, breath shallow. "They're both wearing coats. That's good. I learned a thing about that in a self-defense class I took after... you know." She shook it off in a heartbeat. "Anyway, yeah. Doors."

I observed the movements of Helpful Kid and could hear the click as some part of my brain switched on, one that didn't exist or didn't function before I got the Big Bite, and I started plotting attack vectors. "They're new so they're probably stronger than the ones I dealt with but those guys were pretty weak. They mostly seemed to operate on shock and awe." Jennifer nodded at me in silent agreement. I drew another breath. "Roping zombies. I'm sure there's money in that at a rodeo somewhere." I couldn't help but grin. I'm never so happy as I am when I have a fight on my hands. "Okay, here comes one now. On the count of three."

Jennifer and I both counted – her up, me down, both of us using her heartbeat as the clock without even thinking about it – then she mashed the big red button and the doors threw themselves open. Smiles and I shot at preternatural speed through the first doorway, and then the second, and the air for a growl had just hit my voice box when all three hundred fifty pounds of me nailed Helpful Kid in the shoulder and I body-surfed him across asphalt for ten feet, blood smearing behind us, Smiles sailing through the air at my shoulder the whole way in one continuous leaping glide before landing on the back of the kid's legs with a clatter of thuds.

The smell of fresh blood did wonders for my enthusiasm.

Helpful Kid was slow by my standards but he was strong – just as strong as an athletic youngster can possibly be, dead or otherwise, shockingly so – and his eyes were rolled so far back I couldn't see anything of his irises. He twisted up his fingers like claws and tried to get his arms raised but I was already standing and had him by the shoulders. I picked him up, spun him over to face the pavement and slammed him back down in one fluid motion. Smiles wrapped his jaw around the back of the guy's neck to hold him in place and I popped both of his shoulders out of their sockets with a heartless twist: there would be no standing up under his own power now.

For all her intensity, Jennifer was only human and so vastly slower than I am when I've worked up a head of steam. She took a left as she came out the doors, bat in hand, but by the time she spotted the other lady there was an ear-splitting shriek: a middle-aged man had Phone Lady attached to his forearm and he was screaming like a mezzo soprano, eyes wide, as blood shot in thin jets from the corners of Phone Lady's mouth.

I realized that the one thing I had never witnessed on Z Day, for all the many zombies I killed and all the houses I cleared and all the dead I stepped over on the way to making sure my home, at least, would be safe and sound for another night, was the sight of a zombie actually *biting* someone. I hadn't even been sure they did that. I mean, that's straight out of the movies, right? The things I fought that night killed plenty of humans but they never seemed to try to eat any of them.

It was unexpected and I hate the unexpected.

"Containment?" Jennifer said with visible skepticism and we both moved. I charged directly at Phone Lady but Jennifer was standing right there with the bat already raised and something in Phone Lady recognized her as the more proximate threat. Phone Lady's mouth opened, the guy jogged backwards three steps in terror and then her tongue lolled out in a way that said "bite" in a clear, distinct voice. Jennifer was bringing her bat around for a swing but she would be too slow and I could tell better than anyone else. I shot like I'd been fired from a cannon with all the speed the blood can give me to throw an arm up between them, moving fast enough to be on top of Phone Lady before she could suffer whatever instinctual recalcitrance had made them evade me that night years ago.

Phone Lady's teeth clamped down on the sleeve of my jacket and then, to my utter shock, tore through and hit skin and broke that, too, with a strength that I would never have expected from her. Ancient, stagnant blood the color of an old bruise welled up at the corners of Phone Lady's lips as the pressure of her bite forced some of mine into her.

I had mostly just intended to get in front of her but I was already bringing my other arm around in a punch that connected with enough force to knock

Phone Lady's mouth open. I pulled my arm free and stood back a step fast enough to be out of the way when the end of Jennifer's bat arced past flawlessly in cinematic slow motion and touched that little dip in Phone Lady's temple. I saw blood shoot from the opposing ear before she spun in the air and smacked against the pavement.

Smiles skidded up short in front of me, sniffing the air. The growl was gone but he seemed afraid to approach, unsure what to make of this disabled enemy. We were all silent for a long second. I looked up and Jennifer was staring at my arm, then at me. She started to say something but Phone Lady preempted the conversation by puking her guts out abruptly all over the sidewalk.

You might recall that I can eat mortal food but that most of my kind can't, that our bodies reject it. There are even stories among my kind of Plague Feasts: when a vampire would become frightened that their feeding pool were carriers of some sickness or another, anything that might infect them, they would order an enormous banquet of mortal food prepared and then eat it all in one very long sitting. The vampire would use the consumption of food as a purgative over and over again until their paranoia was satisfied or their guts were sore from effort. What fewer of us know is that the same is true for mortal creatures that consume the blood of a vampire. A human or an animal eats food to stay alive but drinking the blood of a vampire – something with all sorts of benefits in the long run – takes many tries and a great deal of patience and effort. That transaction, the consumption of blood to sustain rather than to sicken, is a one-way street. Human bodies reject our blood just as terribly as we reject their food until they've been trained to it. Phone Lady clearly had not been trained and her body seemed to purge itself thoroughly in one horrible convulsion. Jennifer let out one long, low breath in a ragged, moaning sigh and I detected in it something of the knowledge it might be her job to hose this bit of parking lot down in twenty minutes.

Before Jennifer could say anything about the bite I turned to the guy, who had stopped screaming when the lady's teeth got yanked out of his arm, and said, "Okay, buddy, it's gonna be alright. The cops are already on their way, so, like, they'll bring an ambulance or whatever."

The guy stared at me – no, past me – and then his eyes rolled back in his head and he collapsed in a faint. I clucked my tongue in pity. I couldn't blame him.

"Listen, folks," I said, looking around at the group, all the rest of whom had gone still and silent once Jennifer and I tore ass into the middle of everything. "Let's just stay calm and wait for the authorities to deal with this."

Then the guy stood again, right beside me, with his eyes still rolled back and foam at the corners of his mouth.

So did the other six or seven people who'd originally been knocked out by the lady's gas attack. They were all staring at the insides of their own skulls and their hands all twitched and they produced a collective groan that sent chills up even *my* spine: their voices joined in a chorus that formed an agonized and wordless chant we all recognized from a hundred midnight movies, something they had never done before.

Everyone started screaming at once as the new guys started biting anyone who'd hold still for it so by the time Jennifer and I had dragged each other back inside there were at least a dozen zombies, some of them inside and some of them out and one of them had dragged herself across the path of the sliding doors so the red button wouldn't do anything when we screeched past it and slammed our hands on it five or six dozen times.

I was moving at the maximum speed I felt would be believable when all this store footage got examined, so Jennifer and Smiles were easily keeping pace. I got the sense Jennifer was holding back, actually, so I sped up just a fraction and she changed pace to match me without even noticing. We were at the front of the pack by a long shot and there were people getting taken down behind us as the rest of the survivors strung themselves out into a long chain twisting around corners and down aisles between the front door and us. We would hear someone scream and then abruptly stop screaming and know what had happened. The bad news was that it kept happening, as though these zombies, unlike the shuffling, shambling corpses I'd dealt with before, were pretty quick on their feet, perhaps even faster than a really frightened human being riding an abrupt adrenaline high.

We rounded a corner past a sign that read in absurdly bright letters, "SPECIAL OCCASION!!!" Jennifer held up a fist and gave some sort of signal that I guessed was another part of her self-defense training or something, or maybe something she'd seen on TV, I couldn't begin to know, but she was stopping so I stopped as well and Smiles automatically took up a position at the end of the aisle, watching the direction from which we'd come. "Show me your arm," she said.

Vampires heal fast. I held up my arm and auditioned a nonchalant chuckle. "Didn't break the skin. Lucky me." Jennifer looked at my arm for a long moment, visibly chose not to say something and went on while wearing a mask of passivity that clearly concealed the mechanism of an impressive mind working underneath. "We have to start taking them out," she said. She was only barely breathing hard. She'd been training. I don't mean she jogged around the block on weekends, either. I mean she'd been training intensely and my money was on her having started the day she woke up and realized (a) her initial traumatic event was really over and (b) there was no reason to assume it could never happen again. There's a certain way people react to trauma sometimes, and it's to train like they're about to get to go back in time and kick that one really bad day right square in the pants. It's kind of like how the children of alcoholics grow up to be drunks but with less drinking and more, you know, ropes courses and marathons. I don't know if that's healthy or not but it's something I've seen a hundred times. Vampires are usually living in some version of yesterday in a hundred different ways and that's just a part of the deal but there's something about seeing it in a mortal that's particularly sad.

Regardless, I really, really did not want to get into a direct engagement with a bunch of zombies because I knew what they would do in any circumstance other than one of total surprise like I'd just enjoyed: they would shy away from me by instinct and I would be outing myself as something other than a normal human being. I'd set up the bull rush of Helpful Kid and jumped in front of Phone Lady the way I did precisely to deny them the chance to react to me in the first place but I couldn't ambush all of the ones we had now. Those cameras up there, all over the store, pointed at every nook and cranny where a kid might try to shove an Atari down his pants, could be the start of a hundred nasty questions when someone finally looked at this footage. I couldn't afford that; I was pushing it already with the running and tackling I'd done. But maybe if I could catch the first few walkers, the ones that were moving easier than the rest, at least I could do something to help the odds of everyone else. I nodded at her. "Okay. I kind of have an idea." My hope was that if I would go mix it up with the ones in front that the ones behind them might stop short rather than get too close to me. It would be risky but if I was fast then I could maybe open a tiny window of time for everyone else to go somewhere and hide. "But you're going to need to get everyone else someplace safe."

"I can get them into the back and lock the doors to the storeroom." Jennifer nodded. She hadn't had time to think this through but she didn't need it; she'd already thought it through a hundred times. "You'll need weapons." She held out the baseball bat.

I shook my head and held up two fat fists, my knuckles like dimples in the flesh of a soft white face. "I've got these, and him." I nodded at Smiles. "We've done this before and we've got some good tricks."

She didn't like that answer and her jaw set hard. She looked from me to Smiles — this dog that reacted as though I'd issued orders before I'd had a chance to issue them and who moved like some extension of my own senses — and then back to me. "Tell me what you are."

"Later."

Jennifer's expression didn't change. "To hell with later. Tell me. You tried to screw with my head. You screwed with my boss' head. I saw that woman bite you and I saw blood come out but there's not the tiniest mark now. The others got converted immediately but you're up running around and talking and everything. You're something special, aren't you?" Her glance flicked out and we could hear the screams of some of the other shoppers being picked off closer now. Pounding feet would stop and scuffle and then turn into purposeful steps after a few moments of horrible silence.

I cut her off at the logical pass. "I'm not like them, no."

"No, but you aren't like me, either." She shook her head. "Tell me now or I start screaming and draw them here faster. I swear to God I will get everyone in here killed by the enemy I know before I'll trust the ally I don't and I know exactly how to get their attention. I've done it before."

I made a mental note of that, but outwardly I simply sighed at her and slumped against the shelf of wrapping paper and ridiculous bows and an over-packaged piece of plastic shaped so that it could be used to curl a ribbon.

"I'm… it's complicated." I looked back at the cameras. "I'm something that they can't be allowed to see."

"Ghost?"

I gave her that *oh-honey-please* look every Southern queen keeps in a holster on his hip. "Because so many damn ghosts weigh three and a half bucks and go shopping on Black Friday, right? Trust me, I'm just like you."

"You just fought two zombies and ran approximately three hundred yards. You wear jeans with a fifty-inch waist. You aren't sweating. You aren't breathing hard. Your hair isn't mussed. Your pupils are not dilated. Your dog is not normal. You are not human."

We both blurted out at once, her to make the point, me to answer it: "I can't do this by myself!" We both immediately froze in the stark light of having opened up enough to ask for help. Jennifer breathed in once, held it, let it out. I didn't. She blinked and her features twitched; she'd noticed.

We were facing each other, slightly crouched, hunched like the founders of a conspiracy. I was trying hard to keep a lid on my emotions in this circumstance but Jennifer's insistent curiosity wasn't helping any. That part of me that yanks at its leash when life becomes in any way stressful or demanding was straining against the chain with all four paws dug in the dirt. I started to say something to break that moment of terrifying vulnerability – I don't even know what words I had in mind – when something moved in one corner of my vision, way off at the far end of the aisle, the one where Smiles was not. I just caught one curve of an ear and part of the iris of an eye before it was yanked back out of view.

We were being hunted and they were stealthy enough for me not to have heard. That had never happened in my many years of life despite having been hunted before.

I didn't care that my fangs had fallen out all over the place when I pulled back and hissed at Jennifer. "I came here to buy a Blu-Ray player because my cousin said to," I spat, "But I'm worse than a hundred of Them put together and I swear on every ounce of blood in their bodies that if one thing walks out of here tonight it will be me. Now get everyone who's still clean into the back room and lock yourselves in because I am about to make a mess of this place." Smiles' head snapped around to look at me for one moment before he bounded into position between us in a single leap.

Jennifer looked at me, at my teeth, and blinked in slow motion before she stepped out of the aisle and picked up a bright orange telephone handset from a price check thing on the end of the shelving. ATTENTION ÜBERBARGAINS SHOPPERS, she said in a booming broadcast. I shook my arms back and forth and tried to calm down. My teeth wouldn't go back in. It wouldn't work. I had been pushed right up to the edge of something; some psychological chasm I didn't know was there and hadn't been prepared to leap. PLEASE PROCEED TO SEASONAL GOODS AT THE BACK OF THE STORE. I NEED EVERYONE INTO THE BACK RIGHT NOW. I'LL BE BY THE DOUBLE DOORS BEHIND THE DISPLAY OF CHRISTMAS TREES IN THIRTY SECONDS. REPEAT: SEASONAL GOODS, DOUBLE DOORS, THIRTY SECONDS. NOW. RUN FOR IT.

Jennifer set the telephone thing back in its cradle and took off running again without looking back. I ran the other way, arms outstretched, through the middle of a major traffic aisle and then cutting the corner through Active Wear and Big & Tall. Smiles bounded around a rack of gym shorts and burst through a cardboard display of cheap t-shirts. I cried out as we ran, with a note of sincere joy amidst all the worry and doubt and a little bit of fear: "Heeeeeeeere zombies! Come and get it! Dinner bell's a'ringin'!" The freedom of a fight was something I desperately needed and I was finding it harder to care about the cameras by the second.

The only people who were still up and running from the growing number of walkers in the front half of the store were the younger or fitter members of those of us who'd been lined up outside to begin with. It looked like everyone who hadn't been fast on their feet had been caught and bitten and I watched as one went through a very brief seizure of some sort and then stood up to join the rest of the mob. It was terrifying, to be honest, to watch someone be turned like that into something so mindless; dull, even. I think that's what bothered me about walkers when I saw them in my neighborhood, too. There are vampires who see their transformation as an act of archival more than anything else: the preservation of themselves as an instance of direct experience and intellect, encased in an everlasting vehicle that was once the body of their mortal self. I don't quite view it that way, myself. I've never been totally comfortable with metaphysics based on there being a soul distinct from the body but I've never been a total nihilist, either. I value this life because I get to keep watching the world and depicting it in art and memorializing everything that's ceased to exist and experiencing the new when it arrives but I'm not sure it's more complicated than that for me or for most of us. At some point in most vampires' existences we work to turn off the part of us that might once have contemplated a life after this one. Continuing to care what happens in the great hereafter seems like hedging our bet when the permanence of *this* life is presumably why we signed on in the first place.

Anyway, we place a premium on individuality and the preservation of whatever it is that makes a person *them*. To see that erased in a few seconds was the most terrible thing I'd seen in many years and I see terrible things every time I go out to dinner.

Jennifer's announcement over the intercom had flushed out a few other survivors of the initial outburst from just a couple of minutes before and they were burning rubber towards the back of the store. As we passed one another one of them tried to shout some warning or distraction but I merely yelled at them to keep running and none of them were such devoted humanitarians that they were willing to stop their flight to convince me. I was glad to have them firmly focused on their own survival instead of mine because I didn't want any of them to see what would happen as soon as I got within five feet of one of the zombies and it tried to get away from me. The zombies were advancing in their slow shamble, moaning and groaning, sometimes separately but far too often for my liking it seemed they were trying to articulate something and doing so in *unison*. Smiles was growling like a motorcycle engine being revved in place and I opened my mouth to let out a howl of anger, some animal cry to say that there was a barrier between their turf and mine that they had trespassed, and then I skidded to a stop about ten feet from them.

They walked closer one step, then another, then a third… and then the one in front was within three feet and put a hand on my forearm as though to hold me still. His – *its* – mouth opened and it and all the others around it said, I swear to the gods, "Brains…"

In that moment I realized three things:

First, these things were not at all frightened of me. They lacked entirely whatever instinct the walkers from Z Day had possessed that made them try to avoid me at all costs. They were biting instead of wandering aimlessly around. They were fresh. They'd spoken; I'd have sworn it on a stack of Bibles. They were hunting as a group – no, as a pack. They were not consuming their victims: they were converting them. They were not whatever it was that I had fought and killed in so many silent suburban houses years ago while my neighborhood association's executive board tried to decide whether they were more afraid of zombies or of me. These were new, whatever they were, and they were just as happy to try to bite me as anyone else.

Second, I was going to kill every last one of them before I would let them turn me into just another entry on the value menu.

Third, that kid with the fancy phone camera thing was standing twenty feet away filming us when I gave the zombie a fang-ringed hiss, Smiles bit down on the guy's arm to get his hand off of me and I punched the guy in the gut so hard he was knocked free of gravity and both of us, flew twenty feet through the air and slammed into a couple of other zombies coming up behind him.

I turned around to face the kid, still snarling, but he barely flinched. I wondered if a part of him had guided him to watch everything through his phone as a reflexive way of trying to distance himself from events happening at arm's length, like if he watched it on his phone then it must not be real even though he was the one filming it. Oh well, another one for the philosophers.

The active fear on the guy's young face turned into paralyzed terror as I crossed the gap between us in less time than a mortal man could have turned around, fangs still out, no longer giving a damn about any cameras at all. I could figure something out about cameras later. Right now I needed to survive. I ripped the phone from his hand and crushed it in one fist. Glass and plastic and little bits of ridiculously tiny keyboard fountained from my hand like confetti. I was so angry at this person – this mortal child, this human larva – for having decided now was the time to become a YouTube hero. I don't even know why, but I suspect a little of it was feeling like it was an act of offensive ingratitude to get an invitation to safety over the goddamned intercom and instead to decide to start filming? I don't know why I did what I did, but as soon as the last of the camera skittered across the floor I grabbed him by the front of the shirt, spun on my heels and threw him like a shot put so that he landed fifty feet away in the middle of a half dozen walkers who somehow managed to stay upright when he collapsed in their midst.

I realized the rashness and absurdity of what I'd just done the moment I did it but it was too late by then. They reached down for Camera Kid, lifted him by his shoulders and two of them bit down at once. I couldn't look away any more than any of us can look away from a wreck on the side of the road. Blood shot out from between them as they descended on him and the kid screamed to high heaven until one of them clamped a hand over his mouth. He strained against it, eyes bulging, feet kicking in the air until he fell still and went limp in their arms, then convulsed. His eyes fluttered back and in seconds he was standing under his own power as one of Them.

And, I realized, They had changed.

They had stopped walking and stood in place. I could feel something, some essential energy in the air, maybe the psychic white noise of constant hunger and human desire to which a vampire is at first hyper-sensitive and then eventually necessarily deaf, that thrummed for a moment then skipped and resumed at a different pitch but with similar purpose: the sound of an engine changing when the transmission shifts gears. Much as I had heard the phrase "food chain" as an unwelcome, unbidden thought when I was standing in the street in front of the Reinholdts' place that night, a thought occurred to me now: critical mass.

All of their eyes fluttered back down so that their irises were visible again and they blinked. Only a vampire would have noticed or even could have noticed at all, I'm sure, but when they blinked it was as one. They took a step forward, including Camera Kid, and they all looked at me. I could see the musculature of their bodies ripple under their clothes – all of them, young and old, thin and fat, athletes and couch potatoes – as thirty-five of them shifted stance and got ready to run and the only person around was *me*.

They all said, in a whispered chorus that carried just fine by my ears, "What are you?"

Smiles started barking his head off and I screamed to high heaven and the two of us took off running for the back of the store. Fuck the cameras and fuck these guys and fuck everybody and everything: I had to get out of here and so did everyone else who wasn't one of them and everyone who was one of them would simply have to die.

I ran like a train derailing: spinning and churning at the corners, propelled ever forward, incapable of stopping if I'd wanted to. Active Wear and Big & Tall and Maternity and Luggage and School Supplies were just blurs. Jennifer had said she would lock those doors in the back in thirty seconds and that had been something like a minute or a minute and a half ago but I had my fingers crossed that she was assuming the worst of the humanity around her and that she would hold the doors past the announced time like she probably had to do every time she worked the closing shift in a place like this. Seasonal Goods came into view in the distance and I noticed a couple of the Christmas trees and an oversized inflatable menorah were on their sides in the aisles. I hoped that didn't mean things were too crazy, that nothing had gotten back here, that no one was bitten and that Jennifer wasn't hurt. I had a lot of respect for her, going out into the world every night and working amongst people even though she probably woke up screaming all the time from nightmares about the dead rising up out of the middle of them.

With a vampire's ears I heard the locks clank shut at the bottoms and tops of the double doors marked EMPLOYEES ONLY. I screamed something unintelligible but it was too late. Jennifer had done what she'd said she'd do, and then she'd waited a little longer than she'd said she would, and when she heard me screaming she closed up shop to save the people she could. Damn her to all of Dante's circles and some new ones to boot but I liked this human. I liked her for all the same reasons I'd grudgingly liked Mary Lou for staying up all night with a handgun and the television and nothing else.

I could have ripped the doors open, I'm sure, but that would have defeated the purpose. A part of me wanted to do that anyway just to have somewhere else to run, just because I knew there would be an exit back there somewhere, but I didn't let the rising panic take me away like that. I couldn't yet let the teeth take over and start doing *all* my thinking. That was never a good option.

Well, almost never. Instead I kept going and started shooting up and down various aisles in random patterns.

The zombies were pounding along behind me, unable to catch up to a vampire but able to spread out and cover a huge amount of real estate at one time. Had one or two people pursued me then I could have just run zigzags around the store to build distance and confuse them but they had the numbers – and apparently the smarts – to take over a bunch of territory at once and keep me contained as soon as I started trying to do that. I had about a third of the store still ahead of me, still open, when the intercom crackled to life and I heard Jennifer's booming voice.

"PICK UP THE ORANGE PHONE. ANY ORANGE PHONE."

There was no time. I had to do some hurting of people. We could chitchat later.

Cleaning Products appeared on a sign ahead of me, one of the little ones at the ends of the aisle, and I tore down it, arms out, sweeping up one huge bottle of laundry detergent after another. Damn the torpedoes, it was time to fight and to use all my advantages. With Smiles bounding after me, the rest of the world blurred. Over the course of the first airborne twirl in a picture-perfect quadruple lutz I tore the sides out of four of the plastic jugs and let go of them, pointed down, so that concentrated soap could gush out towards the floor.

In the time it took to execute the second spin I grabbed up four more economy-sized tubs of some cleaner or another and flung them behind me at the slow-motion zombies trying to sprint to keep up and doing a better job than any human should be able to do. The chemical cleansers tumbled away from me like that video of that astronaut throwing a baseball in space, the one where it goes so slow he can run ahead of it, pick up a bat and swing at his own pitch.

On the third spin I grabbed two bottles of chlorine bleach and sent them towards the floor hard enough to rip open and explode on impact.

On the fourth spin I crushed a big jug of dishwashing liquid between my hands so that it would spout from the bottle in a textbook perfect arc to land on top of the bleach.

I've spent decades listening to hippies yammer on and on about household cleaners being chock full of dangerous chemicals and I would like to encourage them to keep doing so because they're one hundred percent correct and that kind of information can prove useful from time to time. Whether you're an environmentalist looking to slow down our relentless march towards ecological disaster – and every vampire is an environmentalist because we learn fast to take the long view in every situation that allows us the time – or someone keeping tabs on ways to explain away a sudden debilitating illness, it pays to know what people bring into their homes and inevitably put into their bodies in one form or another.

When I came down for the landing and kept running, thick boot soles squeaking against the tile floor and my trench coat spinning around to settle back in place around me, the first zombie planted a foot in the laundry detergent, took a jug of cleaning solution to the chest from the air and landed on its ass just in time for a bunch of chloramines to be released from a hissing, bubbling mess of bleach and ammonia in the middle of the floor. I heard him give a ragged, strangled cough and thick globs of cleaner sprayed up, away from his impact, like blood spatter in a crime story sponsored by Tide. The first few zombies behind him were no more fortunate but the fifth one around the corner managed to stop and the rest started to divert. They were reacting before they'd even seen it and they were fast, fast like a junkie all cracked out on uppers.

Four down, thirty to go.

Smiles was one length behind me like he's trained to do so that if needed he can leap past to charge someone while I stop short. His claws clattered and sang on the tile and sounded a lot like a knife cutting fabric. The two of us turned a sharp left at the end of the aisle and as I shot past the next one I saw that some of these sprinters were ignoring the detour I'd taken to try to get ahead of me, off to the left, along the main corridor through the back of the store.

They were herding me, like a border collie and a bunch of sheep only the sheep were in charge.

I cried out with a guttural growl that turned into a shout and pushed off with my next footfall so that I bounded eight or nine feet into the air. All the shelving units in the store had a strip of plastic running along the top; I grabbed it in a classic dorsal grip and executed a passable move, the name of which I couldn't remember but it involved swinging my legs up and over the bar sideways. I pushed off, defying the physics of my generous proportions, and flew upwards and over in a slow arc before landing four aisles away in another avenue of tile. Smiles banked off a different shelving unit to swing around and follow me.

Zombie sprinters were working to keep up with me and though I couldn't see them I could hear them coming from both ends of the nearest block of shelves.

Smiles' lips curled back and his teeth were practically vibrating with the force of the growl he produced. His back was to me, mine to his, and I stamped the floor with my left foot so hard the tile vaporized and plasticized shrapnel shot three feet into the air. My heart kicked out a THA-DUP. My hands spread out. The zombies came around both corners and time crawled as I connected my fists with the jawbones of the two in front, sending them backwards into the ones behind them, then spun and kicked a fifth who had tried to push between them. They were all silent and serious and their gaze was steady. They didn't look like they were necessarily *enjoying* this and that made it all the worse somehow.

My foot came down and I twisted, lifting my opposite foot to bring it up in the crotch of some other zombie, maybe one I'd already hit and maybe not. I could see Smiles, his jaws latched high on the waist of one zombie, another falling backwards from some unknown blow he had landed: six more down for now. When I came around from the second kick I had the edge of my coat in my hand and flicked the corner of it up and into the eyes of a latecomer while I drove my knuckles deep into the stomach of another, then shifted my weight and drove a shoulder into the one I'd blinded, then landed on both feet to rebalance.

More of these things came around the corner all the while and I realized real fast that Smiles and I were in it deep. At the same moment I heard the baritone of a record being played too slow and a hollow *thock* from somewhere off to my left. Jennifer came into view, her bat catching a zombie in the chin behind her as she cocked it back for a second swing at the legs of the one in front. The one behind staggered back, the one in front went over in a heap and she let the momentum of the bat carry her around in a circle to catch the one behind her under the arm and lift him clean off his feet.

I had an ally I hadn't expected and in that moment it felt like a real fight.

Talking to humans when time is all sped up is hard as hell and twice as annoying so I let myself slow down until things were more or less one to one. I placed both hands in the chest of a middle-aged NASCAR dad who'd told me he was here to buy some videogame thing for his kids, picked him up by his own flesh and swung him back and forth, once right, once left, once right again, to sweep several zombies out of the way and push them back. "Things get dull back in the storeroom?"

Jennifer was too busy swinging to answer. Her jaw was set just like before, just like when Helpful Kid and Phone Lady first ran mad eyes around their environment as though they'd never seen with flesh, and her pupils were tiny and fixed directly ahead of her. Her arms were stiffer than they ought to be and her knuckles were solid white. I could tell she was holding her breath. Shock is one of the many afflictions I know well in human beings and she was on the very edge of slipping into it, halfway executing some long-imagined plan for Next Time and halfway trapped all over again in the moment that carried off some part of her sanity in the first place, fighting like wild, pummeling strange men and women like she was beating on the bones of memory itself.

I didn't even consider stopping her because it was way too useful.

NASCAR Dad tried to claw at me with fingers half-clenched and he was much stronger than his doughy exterior would suggest but his nails just barely slipped off my unnaturally tough skin after almost catching. His flesh was hot, red hot, like an iron left on or a radiator set too high. There were *so many* of them, and that part of me that has eternal survival as its only priority was fighting out of the simple desire not to have these monsters hold me down and sit on me until the sun rose outside, nonsensical though that might have seemed had I said it aloud. A couple more sweeps of his body as he kicked his feet and a few more sick thuds of aluminum bat against flesh were enough to clear the field between Jennifer and me. Her bat kept swinging as her eyes searched for a target. I twisted to throw NASCAR Dad through the air, over Smiles. My intention was to use him to knock over a few more but there weren't any standing right there. Smiles had his back arched and his teeth bared but the zombies were all starting to fall still and just wait, watching us. I spun back around and the ones I would have gone after next had backed off, too. They were choosing not to fight me. They were turning to focus on Jennifer.

"Jennifer," I said, but she wasn't listening. She was just swinging at the already fallen, beating the beaten while her fresher foes regrouped and retargeted. I clicked my cheeks and Smiles spun to join me. With two steps I closed the gap between Jennifer and myself, caught her bat in one hand and shook her shoulder with the other. "Jennifer!"

She blinked, her pupils shuddered, and she caught herself. "What did you say?"

"Did it get too boring in the back or something?"

Her eyelids drooped. "No."

"Oh." Zombies were squirming atop one another, trying to get back up all around us and the ones still standing were flowing around it to try to close off Jennifer's egress. I wrapped one arm around her waist. "Time to get some space."

I squatted, pushed and the two of us leapt like a shot from an artillery gun, coming down hard forty feet away on a sturdy unit designed to display kitchen stools and cut-away diagonals of other furniture. I kicked them off, all but one, and set Jennifer down. She had remained silent when I'd expected her to scream or cry out or maybe even shout with joy when we leapt so far from a standing start. Smiles had to cross the distance on the floor but it was no trouble for him to get up to us in a couple of impossibly long bounds. Jennifer ran a hand through her mussed hair and sat down on the remaining stool. We were easily a dozen feet above the ground but she didn't seem to notice or care. I got her to look at me and asked, "Are you okay? Have you been bitten?"

She shook her head vaguely and a quick glance confirmed that she seemed clear. I spoke again before she could fade out. "How bad was it in there?"

"I don't know. One got in but she didn't attack anyone until after I'd locked the doors. She waited. She waited until I'd locked us in. I was still standing there waiting to see if anyone knocked. I let myself back out to get away and heard you fighting so I came to help." She swallowed dry air, her throat working to get it down.

"Did you call the police?" She was starting to stare off into space and I couldn't afford to have her slip into shock so fast. I snapped my fingers in front of her and made her look at me again. "Did you call the police?"

"No. No chance. I locked the doors and then she was attacking people and I came back out and started swinging at the first thing I saw." She let out a rocky, uneven sigh. "I'm sorry."

I smirked. "Don't be. I think I've joined your team now. I say we kill everything we can. We just have to work out a way to separate enough of them at a time to avoid getting overwhelmed. Divide and conquer. Easy-peasy."

Jennifer smiled and it was the saddest twist of a mouth I'd seen in decades. "Do you think we can fight them all?"

"You saw me down there. I'm as good as five men and with you that makes half a dozen. I think we're going to be fine as long as we're careful and observant." Smiles chose that moment to bark once, a sharp shot of warning. Jennifer and I both looked down. We were surrounded on all sides by the horde; many of them battered and bruised, some bleeding, some hobbling on broken legs or letting broken arms hang at their sides. Helpful Kid was even down there, arms limp; somehow he'd managed to get his feet under him and run around with the rest. They were standing there in silence except for their breathing. Every face was turned up, eyes on us, expressions blank. Thirty five of them, pressed close in the aisles on either side and clustered at the ends, like fans at a rock concert only perfectly still.

Lips moved all over the crowd, as though one voice were jumping from mouth to mouth. It said three words:

What
Are
You?

"I don't understand." Her voice wasn't shaking, but Jennifer was quiet. She had tremendous emotional control. I had screamed like a child minutes earlier when they first spoke but she hadn't, now, when they were clearly and indisputably communicating. It occurred to me how exhausting it must be for her to maintain that mask all the time. Anger was probably the only emotion she let herself show and only then for its power to drive people away. Vampires do it all the time: we become the irascible old neighbor everyone avoids, the mean lady in the apartment upstairs, the punk with all the piercings who chain smokes outside the gas station like he's daring someone to say hello. It can be terribly lonely. A human might have had any number of reactions to her: pity, annoyance, dismissal, empathy. As a vampire all I felt was respect.

"They aren't talking to you," I said.

There was a long silence and again she broke it. "Are you going to answer them?"

I licked my lips and looked down. Smiles was standing next to me, his tail up, his ears down. He wasn't growling but he was watching them closely, his eyes shifting from one to another as he tried to protect me from all of them at once. "No," I said, "But I'm willing to answer you. This is as close to 'later' as we might get."

So, I told her what I am. I told her about being a struggling young painter with a bachelor's degree in Fine Art and no marketable skills and a dead-end retail job right out of college in the middle of a booming post-war economy. I told her about my maker, Agatha. She runs a chunk of Atlanta these nights. We talk on the phone. She sees me as an asset and an heir and a trophy all at once since I run things here in the Triangle and a bunch of the rest of the state. I see Agatha as a source of information, a confidante, occasionally as something not entirely unlike an ally. I've never seen her as a friend *per se* and I doubt she would want me to. I told Jennifer about my family, that collection of people with whom I'd rarely shared more than genetics and who hadn't minded seeing me go when I was gone. I'd told Agatha that they would never miss me, never look for me, but Agatha had killed them anyway. That was one of the rules for our kind: it's impossible to leave no trail behind so we do the next best thing by leaving no one to follow what trail we make. I told her how many decades ago it had been and that I couldn't really remember the faces of those people when I tried even though I saw them in the backgrounds of dreams almost every day. They'd become the "magic eye" posters of memory: an optical illusion I couldn't detect when staring directly at it but that worked every time when caught in my peripheral vision. I didn't regret their deaths but I didn't celebrate them. They were like characters in the biography of someone else, some other Withrow Surrett who'd died in 1947, his life and memories left as an inheritance to me. There had been a few people whose existence I'd been able to hide from Agatha and a couple of them were still alive but we didn't exactly see each other often. I told her about cleaning out my neighborhood and wiping the minds of the other members of the neighborhood association so that they would forget what they had learned about me but leaving in everything about the zombies. I told her about choosing to live apart and at the same time amongst the human beings around me. I told her about gay bars in the '40s and how Agatha won me over by accepting me for who I was at a time when none of us received that from someone outside. I told her about having to learn to eat food again and pointed out what just a taste of my blood had done to Phone Lady. At the end, when I was done, I realized that when I said it all out loud my biography sounded sad and strange but to me it was just one night that followed another while I wandered along killing time.

Jennifer was silent throughout and the zombies stood perfectly still as though they strained to listen as well. When I finished I sat there, staring at them, then looking at the clocks in a display at the end of an aisle. It was barely 12:25. It felt like hours had passed but it had only been a few minutes. Where were those damned cops already? Surely one of the people who'd gotten away would have called. People called 911 over nothing these days. It's one of my favorite gripes.

"That's why I didn't want to do anything heavy on camera," I finally said. "I can't let myself be caught doing, you know, vampire stuff. These guys were supposed to avoid me. That's what happened last time. They just ran away when I approached. It made catching them into a little game." I shuddered. We're no more immune to fear than anyone or anything else in the world. After another second I said, "So tell me your story."

After a pause, she did. She told it to a point in the air somewhere, a few feet away, but she told it. Jennifer talked about the crap college where she'd worked and the way she'd burned down her own job to save all those people who'd been such dirt bags to her and to each other. She told me about coming back and working at an ice cream place and waiting to get into a program that never quite seemed to have room for her; about being on a waiting list for years while she floated from one terrible job to another to pay the bills; about getting into running as a way to pass the time and then lifting weights and never realizing that she had started training for something. She told me about her boyfriend who had drifted farther and farther from the center of the frame until one day he peeled off entirely because she'd closed off from everyone else in pursuit of a moment that was already gone: that instant right before the zombies showed up. Even the professor she'd run around with had stopped having much to do with her eventually because all she could talk about was what had happened to them, and she knew it was a problem, but she couldn't stop and she couldn't afford a shrink. She told me about watching her career disappear down the hourglass of time along with all the other sand, about there being no one who needed someone to do the things she knew how to do and never being able to get in the door of the programs that taught something new instead. Her intellectual life was slowly bleeding to death from a thousand tiny cuts: mean customers and mannequin dressing and hauling carts inside. She said she needed a reboot but this wasn't what she'd had in mind: that this was a rerun, not a reboot.

Eventually she stopped talking and we sat there in silence. "I'm sorry," I said.

"Everybody's sorry," she replied. "But that doesn't make the nightmares go away." She cleared her throat. "I have a theory." Her voice had a hint of renewed energy and focus. She was done talking about herself; even zombies were a more pleasant subject. "Is it me or are these guys super-powered?"

I reluctantly concurred with a quiet nod before I spoke. "They're faster than a normal person. They're way stronger than zombies were before. There's something different about them."

"It's kind of nuts, but it could explain a lot." I waited. She went on. "What if the stuff in the can is affecting their brains? I'm a system administrator, not a biologist, but I have a friend who is, or at least he was the last time we talked." She shook something off then, the shadow of yet another connection to her life from before that she'd shoved out a door on her way to the lonely here and now. "He once told me that metabolism is kind of like a computer's CPU." I looked blank. She looked frustrated with me. "It's kind of like a clock for the computer, or a timing chain for a car. Anyway, maybe the gas has affected their bodies' clocks. They're stronger and faster because their bodies are in overdrive. Maybe it's their adrenal glands, I don't know, but there aren't a lot of good ways to end up like this." She drew a breath. "Basically, I'm worried that since they weren't dead to begin with that they're still alive; further, that if they stay like this for long they're just going to fall over dead. It happens sometimes. I read in a book about people who were taking injections of various hormones to amp up their metabolisms – growth hormones, that kind of thing, for stupid reasons – but they did it so much they basically cooked themselves from the inside out." She shuddered. "That might be happening to them, right now."

"They're hot," I said. "Their skin. It's too warm. It's like they're all running a high fever. Is that also what's making them…" I shuddered. "You know, act like they're one person with dozens of bodies?"

She shrugged. "That's something else. Maybe. Probably? I don't know, they're unique somehow. Have you ever heard of something called parallel processing?"

I had not, but she explained it. "Think of lots of computers working on one really big problem, in cooperation with one another. They all get a little part of the problem – whatever math it is they're trying to do – and they all do that little bit at the same time. When their output is assembled the problem has been answered but in a tiny fraction of the time it would take one computer to do all the individual parts in sequence. Get it?"

I looked down at the zombies, still staring back at us. "Not really, but I think I understand what you're getting at. I used to watch a lot of *Wild Kingdom* in the middle of the night. Would 'hive mind' work?"

"Exactly," Jennifer replied. "And if that's the case, it might follow that the more of them they make, the more processing power they acquire. Throw in a realization of cost functions and learning from artificial neural networks and you get a self-expanding supercomputer on legs." I looked at her with a look as blank as a chalkboard in the morning. "They get smarter the more of them there are, Withrow. There were only two at first but now there are fifty."

"The nerve gas must…" I fluttered my lips in ignorance and frustration. "I don't know, give them telepathy or something."

"I don't know either. I'm not a neurologist or an expert on Soviet chemical weapons or anything else that matters here but it would make a kind of sense, wouldn't it? If it's affected their brains in some unknown way it could do metabolism, adrenaline, telepathy, anything at all and we have no real ability to predict or control it. I'm just trying to understand it by viewing it through the lenses I have available."

I scratched my nose and then sighed again. "Okay. Hive mind. So let's say that one of these is one fiftieth as smart as a human. Now they are, collectively, as smart as one human. Right?"

"Maybe." Jennifer chuckled darkly. It was one of the only times I ever heard her laugh. "But what if it's more like twenty-five to one, or ten to one or even five?"

"Then they're as smart as two people, or five… or ten."

"Exactly. God, it's *genius*." She sounded like someone waking from a clever dream and pleased to find she remembered the end. "Potential physiological damage aside, think of the evolutionary advantage of shared mental processing. It's a leap forward. An individual's will to survive, their instinct, their reproductive success, all potentially vastly increased or stabilized. A disaster wouldn't necessarily wipe them out, either. If a tidal wave carries off half the village, the other half just has to find more individuals to join to the collective. Maybe two collectives could recombine by adopting one another. I'm no entomologist but I wonder if there's a parallel in any observed hive insects? If only the metabolic rate thing could be controlled." She was silent for a moment and then blinked, eyes wider still. "Hive insects. Oh, of course." Her voice sounded a little distant now, a little dreamy, and a thought I absolutely hated occurred to me for just a moment. I started to shake it away but I couldn't.

"Jennifer," I said, very slowly, "This is not a laboratory. These things are not objects of study. If these things are a little telepathic or something they may try to suggest you do something, influence you somehow, and you need to resist that. I need your help to get out of here, okay? We need each other. I need you to turn off the security cameras so that I can… so that we can make it possible for us to walk out of here and go home. You have to stay objective about this, Jennifer. You can study them later."

To be honest, I didn't give a damn about the academic questions they raised. I was ready to jump down and wade in with everything I had, with teeth and claws and fists and boots and whatever might be at hand – and Smiles certainly seemed to think this was a fine idea – and we had Jennifer on our side and the zombies seemed to have gotten smart enough to get shy about me again and I could use that, I knew I could, because any enemy can be defeated once you can direct their movements. Before I could start to talk through a plan I fell silent because in the distance, at the front of the store, I saw something I would never in a hundred years have expected to see: a resurrection.

Phone Lady came staggering in the front doors of the ÜberBargains with her phone in her hand and my undead ears could make out her every syllable of her endless stream of chatter even as the zombies cried out at Jennifer and Smiles and me, faces upraised and mouths falling open in one unified scream for flesh and blood and everything else that makes a person a person in and of themselves. Phone Lady said into her handset, unperturbed as ever and stumbling only a little as she limped on one bad leg, "I don't know where everyone is but I swear to Jesus that television had better still be here I've got my paper and these bastards are not going to cheat me out of that television you know Susan bought a television for her boyfriend and he doesn't even go to work and I just think it would be so unfair for that jackass to sit there and watch his shows on a nice teevee when Hank has to watch that old thing we've got you know they play the strangest music in these stores sometimes I swear it just sounds like screaming it's probably some of that rock music you know the only people they ever try to make happy anymore are kids and they're all too stupid to appreciate it."

"You can't kill them, Withrow. You *won't* kill them." Jennifer's voice carried over the sudden chorus of zombie desire, shouted into my ear.

"Why won't I?" I shouted back to make sure she could hear me, my eyes searching for hers but finding that she was looking down at Them. She didn't answer me; instead she slipped neatly out of her chair and fell into the waiting arms of a couple of zombies down below. I reached out with all my speed and tried to catch her but just tore at her shirt instead. By the time she was on the floor their teeth were in her, her eyes were rolling back with the transformation and I was holding hard plastic in my hand. It was her nametag: JENNY.

I was on my feet without thinking about it, arms out, trench coat open and I roared like I haven't in a lot of years – more years than that since I've done it in front of a crowd. The zombies screeched back in answer, a mass of curdled sound bouncing off all the tile and concrete in a big box like that. One of the zombies near me started ambitiously trying to climb the shelving unit but he was clumsy and slow at that particular task and I was fast and very angry. I reached down in a great sweeping arc to snatch him up off the ground in my hands and then ran down the center of the shelf to slam its forehead against the structural pillar at the other end. Blood spattered thickly in two directions. I dropped him like a sack of potatoes on the floor and turned around to see three more trying to clamber up the shelf. The doors to the storeroom flew open and another fifteen or twenty zombies marched out. I do mean *marched*. They were organized, and they were all already looking at me. One mind with forty or fifty bodies was watching me from all sides and it wanted to make me a part of it. The animal inside tore at the psychological fencing I'd built around it for decades. Neither it nor I wanted all that I am to dissolve away in a solution of Them. Whatever sameness infected them could never be allowed to take me.

I roared again and ran back down the shelf to bull rush those three climbers back off of it then take a flying leap across the gap between aisles and land on the next. I was contemplating the options left to me – kill them all or just keep them busy like this until all that metabolic damage caught up to them like Jennifer thought it might and hope like hell it happened in the seven hours or so I had left before sunrise - when I spun to face the enemy below and found that they were standing stock still, mouths open, but that their collective screech was dying off slowly, one voice at a time, and they were falling passive as it happened.

Jennifer stood up in the middle of them. She was staring at her own feet, her hands pressed to her face. My brain was churning as I ran and thoughts started to fall into place. The mass of them produced a mindless syllable, like a cleared throat, and then said as one:

"TE... TESTING."

Jennifer lifted her head out of her hands and blinked. Her eyes were rolled halfway back but the rest of them seemed to be under control. My brain

130

churned and Smiles whined with confusion. Thoughts started to fall into place in my head.

Somehow, Phone Lady had slept it off. It was possible for her to recover. I thought of Jennifer's sad coda to her own biography: that she needed a reboot, not a rerun. They had been breathing while they listened to us. Whatever they were, they were definitely still alive. Jennifer understood complex systems and the processes they used to make decisions, to answer questions put to them, to take orders. Kathy had tried to explain computer programming to us one time, at a board meeting, and I didn't understand a word except that what mattered the most, for her, was to have the process she was trying to manage carefully outlined and her thoughts ordered before she started typing. She said she'd read a book about artificial intelligence in which the author had argued that was the trick: figuring out how people order their tasks and decisions and then reproducing that.

They turned towards me, jerkily, uncertainly, and they all said at once, "You need to feed us to fix us. You need to feed all of us and we need to do this fast."

I jumped down into the middle of them and Smiles came after me, both of us ready to start going at them hammer and tongs, fists and teeth and claws flying. I was so angry and scared that I thought now would be the time to fight, now would be the time when I could take out enough to make it possible to take out the rest. It would feel so good, too, so free. I hadn't felt that in years: that simple pleasure of letting go and allowing the id to drive for a while. I was ready to stand outside myself for a while and take satisfaction in my performance.

They all stepped back, hands up, in a hurry. They – she, whatever – could tell I was ready to brawl. Jennifer dropped the bat on the ground with a clang. "No killing. We can do this. The lady with the phone proves it." They weren't purposefully surrounding me at first but as I hesitated a couple of them moved to do so. "We can fix this together," they said with one voice. "We both said it earlier: neither of us can do this by ourselves." Smiles growled at them and he and I turned in a slow circle, back to back. My eyes were wide. My chest was quivering as my heart twitched in anticipation of blood and shouting. I licked my lips. In unison: "Say something, Withrow. Use your brain. Think. Talk to me."

"It's crazy," I whispered. "It's just crazy. There are fifty of you and you've got her. You think I'm going to hold still and let you bite me?"

"We bit you before," they said. Their voices were low, calm; almost conversational; soothing, even. I blinked and slapped my hands on my own cheeks. I thought of my warning to Jennifer about what they might do if they're telepathic. What if she were right about how it worked, adding more computing power? Now they had her and she was a certifiable genius. "You weren't harmed then, were you? You won't be harmed now. You can fix this, Withrow. We can walk away from another zombie apocalypse and this one can have a body count of zero."

Smiles, very slowly, stopped turning and sat. His tongue hung out and he panted happily. He'd liked Jennifer from the get-go, that was clear, and now he identified her or them-as-her or her-as-them and he'd felt the presence of a threat recede – or they'd done something to his mind with their crazy hive powers. I felt panic start to rise again and they spoke.

"We didn't do anything to your dog. He knows we mean you no harm. We swear it, Withrow. We swear it on…" They paused for a moment. "On the lives and memories of the persons we used to be."

I blinked. That was what I'd pitied and respected in her: that ability to sever herself from the person she'd been before. Now she was here, doing this, braver than ever. The life she'd had before was still recent enough to include names she could say and faces she could remember. It was a life she could go back to, or at least build on, in a way I never would. My fists unclenched. The animal inside started to calm. My teeth still wouldn't go back in but for all that I still felt fear and anger I also felt a wave of sympathy I hadn't experienced in a lot of years. Jennifer would have made a tremendously dangerous vampire. I couldn't let the fearless human she already was be washed away like this.

"What if…" I cleared my throat. "What if one bite didn't hurt me but twenty do? Or forty nine?"

"It doesn't stand to reason," they said.

"On what fucking basis do you say that? Don't yank my chain."

They were quiet for a moment. "Point taken, but it's the only option we've got."

"Now, yes, it is, isn't it? But there were other options. You forced my hand."

"I saved them, and you, and me. We couldn't fight them and I couldn't watch them die. Neither of us could."

I grimaced with young resentment. "This is so completely unfair," I muttered.

"Says the vampire," they replied.

I spit at the feet of the nearest one and Smiles growled.

"Okay, take it easy," they said. Their hands were all up in a calming gesture again. "Let's just stay rational and work through this. We need to get some of your blood into each of us and we need to do this before I lose track of one of them and it goes crazy."

I blinked. "Is it... is it just you in there?"

"No, but I'm the one giving orders." It was just her voice now. "And I can't do that forever, so get to it."

I ran through scenarios in my head again: start fighting, run away, all kinds of things. None of them took care of all the things I still had to square away in order to go back to my home and wake up in it tomorrow and have the years and decades roll on ahead of me without a lot of problems. I didn't care about being a hero to these assholes, this random cross-section of every chump and moron who'd been willing to give up time with their families or the game or whatever so they could squat outside a discount store in hope of getting their paws on some precious little *thing* and I didn't feel any motivation to be a savior to them or to anyone.

"We can save them, Withrow," they said together to me. "Think how glad their families will be. How would you feel if this happened to your cousin? You mentioned a cousin. There are people you still care about and who care about you."

My cousin, the one who'd wanted me to get the Blu-Ray player tonight, had probably been calling me to no avail the whole time. He would want to know if I'd gotten it, maybe to talk me through hooking it up. Roderick is better in some ways than I am at living in the future. He's also a complete monster. The things I do to get by are survival, mostly; for him, immortality is a game of cow tipping that will never end. It seems like for him people are just toys to be played with until they break. I had told myself years ago I'd never be like him, but here I was, thinking of these people like something less than myself. Of course, they were, but maybe that still didn't make it right. I wouldn't feel good about something like this happening to Roderick but that argument couldn't sway me. Reminding me of the little tragedies and petty crimes that added up to becoming Roderick, however? That gained a foothold in my mind.

"Withrow," they said, and they sounded worried. "Withrow, we need to do this. Now. They are fighting back and most of them are kind of idiots but there are a whole lot of them."

Sheep or wolves every time and it's always a toss up. Very tentatively, ready to pull away and start killing at a moment's notice, I slid the long black coat off my shoulders and held out an arm.

Teeth punctured my flesh and my stale, stagnant blood welled up from the pressure and directly into the mouth of the zombie-person who'd bit. It was Jolie, my friend with the cat-hoarding mother. In the long chain of dietary habits found in nature most predators are also, eventually, the prey. For us, that's supposed to be impossible. That's essentially the trade we make: that we're willing to give up everything human to become the next highest thing on the ladder. We give up a lot when we make that deal but every morning when we climb into the dark place where we sleep instead of walking outside to see one last sunrise we reaffirm that choice. We make it over again every time we go out, every time we feed, every time we start the work of building our next identity in the world of the living.

The last time teeth had punctured my flesh before tonight they were the fangs of my maker. She had given me the gift of ultimate and eternal *self* with painful but surgically precise wounds and an arcane ritual I'd never asked to learn. These teeth were the dull, grinding bones of a mortal but they worked almost as well. I struggled against it, flinching of course, but though we're extremely strong, much stronger than a human or even several humans, we are not infinitely strong. Too-warm hands clutched me from all around to hold me in place. Smiles abruptly howled the longest, highest-pitched baying I'd ever heard from him and some of them swarmed him though they didn't seem to want to do anything but hold him back. He struggled but they were strong and for all that Jennifer claimed to be fighting to maintain control they were remarkably precise as they balanced force against a clear desire to do no lasting harm.

The first one to bite me, though, Jolie, she was frozen again just like Phone Lady and Helpful Kid had been when the gas grenade went off and in one coughing gush she emptied her stomach at the others' feet and then collapsed on the ground, unconscious. It was like I'd given her a Plague Feast of her own. The bite wound on my arm healed over in two seconds. We don't stay injured for long. It was one of the hardest moments I'd ever faced but I kept my cool and drew a long, unsteady breath before slowly looking around at the rest of them. "C'mon, folks," I said, voice low. "Dinner bell's a'ringin'." Another six or seven were on me in a moment and as one would sicken and peel away another would immediately take its place, like mad piglets on a pale sow.

Throughout I could hear Phone Lady. She'd made it back to the right part of the store and picked out her television and now she was leaning on the Customer Service button trying to get some help. A cheery voice with a tone carefully modulated to suggest an industrious work ethic and a mountain of submissive goodwill kept announcing, "A customer requires assistance in Electronics!"

The more of them that bit me and dropped the slower they got but the easier it seemed to be for Jennifer to control them so that by the time I'd whittled them down to about two thirds of their starting numbers their eyes started rolling back up into their heads. Jennifer's nearly did but she closed her eyes and clutched the sides of her head, dropping to one knee in the middle of them as though it had gotten difficult again. They kept biting me but faster, harder, like she was trying to push them through this as rapidly as possible. Another fifteen or so had bitten me, gulped down clotted blood and then puked it back out when I realized I was starting to run low. I stood away from them and put up my hands.

"Wait," I said. "I... I'm running out." I shivered hard. "I need to feed on someone."

They paused and their voices were slurred. "Fast."

I reached down and picked up one who'd been out for a while, sniffed his skin and then looked at the ones still standing. A vampire feeds in front of their maker and sometimes at a feast we feed around others of our kind with whom our relationships are somewhat less intimate but to feed in front of other prey felt wrong somehow. I started to tell them to turn their backs, then spun and turned mine instead. My fangs were practically aching and I plunged them into the left side of the poor bastard's neck. The blood was more satisfying than I know how to explain. It always is. It's like you're always just about to drown and then along comes a vein and it's full of wet, delicious air. It was a struggle not to drain him dry on the spot but I managed to push him away from me before he'd die, probably, and wiped the back of my hand across my lips. His blood was hot, salted lightning and all the hair on the back of my neck stood up as it warmed me and the room felt colder in contrast. I blinked fast a dozen times. I wanted more, of course; we always do. There's no such thing as enough blood. There's only the quantity we get before we can make ourselves stop.

"Faaaaaster." It was a groan. Jennifer was struggling, perhaps to keep herself from slipping into whatever catatonia had taken the rest of them at first. I spun around, ripped one of my own fangs down three inches of my forearm and wrapped my opposite hand around the back of a random store employee zombie's head to press its lips to the wound. A flex of muscle shot blood into its mouth. The usual reaction happened but I had already shoved him out of the way and grabbed the next closest, and then another, and then another, stepping around and over the filth of thirty or more humans and all the waste their bodies could produce. It became trivial and then, eventually, boring as I forced my blood into them one at a time.

In the end I was left standing in the middle of fifty unconscious zombies, minus one, and a tremendous mess. Jennifer was the last one up but now she was reduced to some drooling, idiotic fraction of herself. I managed to get some of my blood into her mouth, she puked everywhere and passed out, and two minutes later her eyes fluttered open after I splashed water in her face and patted her on the cheek with one hand. Jennifer yelped and tried to get away and I let her. She shuddered at the sight of all those people on the ground around her and then looked at me. I had my hands up, palms exposed, in the *just a friend, unarmed, my bad* gesture. I had long since healed completely though my clothes were a wreck.

"I…" I couldn't imagine where to begin. "Are you okay?"

She snorted at me after long consideration. "No." She was back in the land of the living and that was all I cared about.

"What made you do that?" I had to ask now, while she was shaken and while the blood made her a little bit suggestible for just a few minutes. "I thought at first you had decided to give up."

"I considered it," she said, "There's nothing left for me. There's nothing new to learn. There's no grad program and no job future and no career. But then there was this, something new, something different. It was an opportunity." She coughed and laughed and shook all at once. "It was a chance to save them and it was a chance to learn something no one else would ever know." She was saying the right things but she was exhausted, visibly so, and the vigor she'd shown before vanished abruptly in the way it only does for people who've scraped up and consumed the very last of their will to fight.

I nodded and then gestured at a shelf. "The lady with the phone and you seem to prove your theory correct but let's get up there just in case." I climbed onto a canopied porch swing, up onto a display of lamps, and clicked my cheeks to summon Smiles up there with me. Jennifer offered me her hand and I pulled her up in one smooth motion. I sat down, tired of beating people senseless, tired of being bitten, a little tired of being alive in a world full of surprises. Smiles settled down with his chin on my knee and panted. I scratched him behind the ears. Jennifer eased into a cross-legged position very carefully. "Do you remember anything from the time you were one of Them?" Jennifer shook her head at something in the distance. I nodded. That was good: lots less explaining to do if they were going to have a little amnesia. Phone Lady rang the Customer Service button again in the distance and I shouted, "SHUT. THE FUCK. UP."

"Somebody in here is getting crazy," she said into her phone. "You wouldn't believe the thing I just heard someone holler well let me just say Jesus doesn't appreciate that kind of talk and neither do I but you hear all kinds of things even at Christmas it's just shameful I don't know why someone who talks like that would even be here it can't be like they have anyone to give gifts you can't talk like that to people can you it's just a tragedy." The contradiction with her earlier diatribe did not seem to register for her; for people like that, it never does.

I sighed heavily, stuck my fingers in my ears and started watching the clock.

The police arrived thirty seconds later, guns drawn, and when the three responding officers came running around the corner they stopped short at the sight of so many badly beaten people. I about scared the pants off of them by speaking from our perch above. "The lady in electronics," I said, my voice weary. "She used some kind of pepper spray thing and flipped out and now she's over there trying to buy a television." I jerked my thumb that way. "Everyone else stampeded and trampled each other senseless. You're going to need a bunch of ambulances."

They blinked at me; at Smiles; at Jennifer.

"Don't ask me, man." I shrugged. "People do some crazy stuff."

"She went bonkers and then they all did." Jennifer said. Her voice was completely leaden. "Groupthink."

The cops took off running in that direction and I turned to Jennifer. "I have a favor to ask."

"The cameras," she said. "I know. Let's go."

We climbed down and walked into the back. Jennifer unplugged some things back there and did some fiddling and then she started hitting some little boxes, very hard, with a big hammer so that pieces of plastic shattered and flew off in all directions. They weren't tapes like I've seen and used and own but she said they were what the video lived on, like little computers. "Trust me," she said. "I just lied to the cops. I don't want them seeing this any more than you do." It wasn't much but I had to trust her. I didn't have a lot of choice.

"Thanks," I finally said. My voice betrayed something, though, and Jennifer got to that can of worms and cracked it open way before I could or would.

"You're debating whether to kill me, aren't you?" She didn't look at me at first, but then she looked up and met my eyes.

I'd been thinking about it. I'd wiped Mary Lou's memories and Herb and Franklin Not Frank and Kathy without a second thought because it had *worked.*

My attempts to screw around with Jennifer's head earlier had failed, though, and there was something about her mind – I could just tell – that would always resist that. I would never be able to wipe her memory or, if I did, I would never be certain it would hold. I couldn't just walk away having told a human my life story, either; especially not a human with as much fight and nerve as Jennifer had. For all I knew she was going to wake up tomorrow and decide she was done training to fight zombies because she was ready to start hunting vampires.

"It would be hard to do with the cops out there reading Phone Lady her rights, wouldn't it? They're probably looking for us by now." I sighed. It was now or never.

"You could blame it on the zombies. Say the gas made someone go crazy and attack me." Jennifer's eyes were cold. She was already dead inside in a way. I might be doing her a favor.

I couldn't do it, though. The cops had already seen her and talked to her and anyway I couldn't let the reward for surviving everything she'd seen and done be to die in the end anyway. I didn't like the idea of a smart, capable, depressed mortal in search of a purpose in life wandering around out there knowing all about me but I couldn't bring myself to snuff her out, either. Maybe it was sentiment or sympathy or something else. Maybe it was weakness.

Maybe it was the formless forgotten faces of the people I'd seen at Thanksgiving when I was alive.

"Maybe next time, Jennifer." I tried to smile. It didn't work very well but it beat everything else I could do. "Happy Thanksgiving."

Jennifer had chosen to risk everything once tonight when she'd given herself over to the zombie horde in order to take it over. She'd done the same when she saved her college by getting every zombie in sight to home in on her and no one else. Now she'd done it again when she come back here and destroyed the evidence against both of us even though she knew I was already contemplating whether she could be allowed to live. They say the third time's the charm and I think this once they were right: something, some spark of spirit, some essential drive to do more than merely survive, sprang up in her eyes and her expression sagged and softened just a little.

"H… Happy Thanksgiving. Withrow." She held out a hand. I took it. We shook once and we each let go. "Do you…." She looked around at nothing.

"How do you do things like this and survive? You must have seen a lot of terrible things. Where did you learn to cope? Can I... can I talk to you sometime? Can you help me figure this stuff out?"

I put my hands in my pockets. "Nope. Get an analyst – a therapist, whatever they're called these days – no matter how much it costs. Find a program that'll help pay for it. Get over it like everyone else. I'm not special for having survived a few things, Jennifer. People do it all the time." I shrugged. "I'm doing that right now. I haven't left a mortal alive with knowledge of me in a lot of years." Her nostrils flared in reflexive fear. "But that's life: a little risk and, if you're lucky, a little reward, right? So I'm choosing to take this risk by walking away. Don't make me regret it and don't try to find me and especially don't disappoint me by going off the deep end. That's all either of us could ever ask."

I turned around and walked away, back out onto the sales floor, right past the cops. They tried to ask me questions but I made them forget I'd ever been there. They had plenty of chaos to clean up and it was easy simply to erase myself from that jumbled mass of impressions. Jennifer must have flipped a switch somewhere because Christmas music started playing. I picked up one of the Blu-Ray players from a big stack that had a flashing orange light on top of it, went outside and opened the passenger door on my old Firebird so Smiles could climb in. I got behind the wheel and drove away. I didn't even consider looking back. I wouldn't have known what to do with a friend if I'd had one.

A little risk, a little reward. They're all anybody ever gets.

EDIBLE INTERLUDE

Icebox Cakes

Icebox cakes are an evolution of the charlotte or trifle, desserts that date from the 16th or 17th centuries. This 20th century version became popularized in the 1920's as a trendy way to make use of the popular, new and eponymous kitchen appliance. They can be made complicated or simply and they can easily be constructed from anything one might find on hand when trapped in a big-box retail store. Icebox cakes can be extremely rich and they are constructed entirely of processed foods, so gods help your guts if you eat a lot of them, but they are quite delicious.

1 package vanilla wafers, sandwich cookies or similar
1 tub whipped topping
1 9x13 or similar baking dish

Place a layer of wafers or cookies on the bottom of the pan and cover with a layer of whipped topping between a quarter- to a half-inch in thickness. Layer more wafers or cookies on top of that, then more whipped topping, and so on until you've used up one or the other. If you wish, you can layer canned pie filling in there, too. Cover with plastic wrap or foil and stick somewhere cold for a few hours. If you're in a store like ÜberBargains then you will find plenty of refrigerated cases you can use.

Let it sit for six to eight hours and the wafers or cookies will absorb the moisture from the whipped topping, becoming enlarged and softening into a texture not entirely unlike a dense cake. Serve with a spoon, with plenty of napkins on hand. At one time the standard was to arrange the cookies to form "logs" and then slice them at an angle, or to use highball glasses and layer the ingredients at an angle, to make them seem a little more chic. In an emergency, skip the presentation in favor of a few moments of pleasure. As the saying goes, life is short: eat dessert first.

ABOUT THE AUTHOR

MICHAEL G. WILLIAMS is a native of the mountains of western North Carolina and has resided in the Triangle area of the state for twenty years. He has been a successful participant in National Novel Writing Month for many years and encourages anyone interested in writing to jump headlong into the deep end of insanity for thirty days. More information can be found at www.nanowrimo.org.

Michael is a brother in St. Anthony Hall and Mu Beta Psi and believes strongly in the power of found families. He lives in Durham with two cats and more and better friends than he probably deserves. Michael earned a BA in Performance Studies at UNC Chapel Hill and works as an engineer. He can be reached via email at michaelgwilliams@gmail.com. More information about *Perishables* can be found at www.perishablesbook.com or at http://www.robustmcmanlypants.org/perishables. The latter is recommended especially to those curious to learn about the process of its publication and future publications.

Twitter: @mcmanlypants
Facebook: http://www.facebook.com/perishables.novel

Made in the USA
Lexington, KY
04 November 2019